SHADOW GIRL

GIRL

BY

PATRICIA MORRISON

TUNDRA BOOKS

Published in Canada by Tundra Books, a division of Random House of
Canada Limited,
One Toronto Street, Suite 300, Toronto, Ontario M5C 2V6

Published in the United States by Tundra Books of Northern New York,
P.O. Box 1030, Plattsburgh, New York 12901

Library of Congress Control Number: 2012938138

Library and Archives Canada Cataloguing in Publication

Morrison, Patricia (Patricia Margaret)
Shadow girl / by Patricia Morrison.

ISBN 978-1-77049-290-5. – ISBN 978-1-77049-368-1 (EPUB)

I. Title.

PS8626.O763S53 2013   jC813'.6   C2011-906501-0

We acknowledge the financial support of the Government of Canada
through the Canada Book Fund and that of the Government of Ontario
through the Ontario Media Development Corporation's Ontario Book
Initiative. We further acknowledge the support of the Canada Council for
the Arts and the Ontario Arts Council for our publishing program.

Edited by Sue Tate and Kelly Jones
Designed by Terri Nimmo

Printed and bound in the United States of America

www.tundrabooks.com

1 2 3 4 5 6   18 17 16 15 14 13

For my children, Gen and Adam

ACKNOWLEDGMENTS

I'd like to acknowledge my readers: Mary Budd, Sheila Cameron, Ashley Frederick, Maria Pucek, and Meera Shah. Thank you to Dalia al-Kury for your belief in Jules from the start, Cynthia Flood and Claire Robson for your wise counsel on literary matters, Sue Tate at Tundra for helping me find my way, Jolanta Kosewska for friendship above and beyond, Sadao Katagiri for your constant caring and support, and my sons – Adam Katagiri, my inspiration, and Gen Katagiri, whose guidance, help, and love carried me every step of the way.

PART ONE **1963**

CHAPTER

1

The sun shone through the window.

December 11. Another million years before Christmas.

Jules leaned over the edge of the bed in order to see outside.

Her bedroom window faced the backyard. The enormous tree she and her friend Patsy often climbed stood just a few feet away. She could almost touch it. The long arms of the branches were still.

A pure winter day. There's something good in that.

During the night, ice had built up on the window. It seemed to form a different pattern every time. Sunlight hit patches of the old lino floor, bringing some warmth to the freezing room.

Jules had put her long stockings in the exact spot where she'd have to put her feet down. She swung her legs over the side of the bed, sat up, and put them on.

She'd slept in her school clothes again – and that wasn't good. She had only one uniform and often got into trouble at school when it looked rumpled and dirty. It was bad enough that the uniform was getting too small. She went into the bathroom to wash her face.

White as a ghost, she was.

Jules's eyes were big and hazel-colored, like her father's. They were the only part of her face that was really different, she figured, because her nose and mouth were normal. Boys in her class were starting to talk about stuff like that.

Ugh.

Jules already knew she was different from other kids, but not in any way you could tell from speaking to her. She just felt different – maybe because she lived differently. Most of her classmates and friends had a home that felt like one, even if they were as poor as Jules and her father.

Maybe he doesn't care about things like that.

It was hard to know how her father felt about anything a lot of the time, though. The nights he came home drunk, Jules would quickly make herself a sandwich for dinner and get to her room as soon as she could. Her dad would yell at her if she got in his way, even though she did everything so that he wouldn't be bothered by her. He'd talk to himself, get some beer from the fridge, and watch TV until he fell asleep.

Once in her room, Jules would turn on the old

lamp that was on the floor near her bed and make a small fort with her blankets, propping them up with pieces of wood she had found in the park nearby. She'd made forts ever since she was little. It didn't matter that she was eleven now and not a little kid anymore. Her blanket fort was her own special place to be. When she was inside it, she could disappear inside her dreams.

Jules wet a facecloth and tried to straighten out the worst wrinkles in her uniform. When she was done, she went downstairs. Her father was under an old blanket, sleeping in his chair. The TV was still on.

She knew it wouldn't be good to wake him up, so she went about her normal routine, pulling the box of Corn Flakes from the cupboard and getting milk from the fridge. She opened the milk carton and took a sniff.

Ew. Can't drink this.

She filled a bowl with cereal and sat down. It was hard to eat dry.

Even though she'd slept for a long, long time, she was tired. It'd be tough trudging through the snow today, getting to school. The whole world outside the kitchen window looked frozen.

She put the bread and margarine on the counter to make a sandwich and then looked in the fridge.

Don't tell me it's lousy Cheez Whiz again!

She took the jar from the fridge and opened it. It didn't smell good, either. And the spread – what was left of it – had dried and was turning brown in some spots. She scooped out what she could and tried to put blobs of it on the bread without making holes. She wished that on days when she brought rotten lunches to school, she could eat them by herself in the school yard so nobody could make fun of her.

Hopefully her dad would have some money tonight when he came home. She needed to get some groceries at the variety store.

Gotta hurry. Gotta see if Patsy's left for school yet.

Jules went to check on her father once more. He was snoring loudly. He probably wouldn't get to work today, and she knew what that meant on payday.

She got her coat, scarf, tuque, and mitts, put on her boots, and left the house quietly.

Swinging by Patsy's house on Martin Grove Road, she was glad Patsy was still there. They walked to their school, Our Lady of Peace, and all they talked about was Christmas.

"What'd you ask for, Jules?"

Jules almost answered right away, but caught herself. "My dad likes to surprise me."

"But what do you *want*?"

More than anything, Jules wanted a doll she'd seen in Zellers at the Six Points Plaza. She didn't know whether or not to tell Patsy about it because there wasn't much chance she'd get it.

But Patsy was her good friend, and Jules knew that Patsy didn't get many gifts for Christmas, her birthday, or ever. Jules was glad her father didn't hate

Mr. and Mrs. O'Connor like he did some of the other families in the neighborhood, the ones who weren't friendly to him. He said they acted like snobs because they were living in a "good" area – even though they ate Kraft Dinner every night.

"I want a doll I saw at the plaza," Jules said. "Do you want to walk over there after school? I can show you."

"Wish I could, but it's my turn to look after Marcus."

Patsy's brother was disabled, and she and her older sister, Rosey, took turns taking care of him after school until their mom and dad got home from work.

"Maybe on the weekend?"

"Sure."

Patsy didn't say Jules was too old for a doll because Patsy still played with dolls herself. And Jules didn't act like a baby. Far from it. She was more grown-up than a lot of kids. Took care of herself. Even took care of her dad sometimes. Most kids couldn't do that.

Patsy loved horses and kept asking her parents for one of her own. And if she couldn't have a horse, she wanted riding lessons.

Jules knew that Patsy's family couldn't afford to pay for any kind of lesson, let alone buy a horse. She could've said, "That'll never happen in a million years," but didn't. They never made fun of each other's dreams.

But Dad can afford to buy a doll. I can pretend the doll's a child, my own little girl to care for, who cares for me back. And when I play with her, I can do what I always do: pretend the world's warm and sunny, not cold and dark. Pretend she needs me, like family.

"We're at Mervyn Avenue," Patsy said, interrupting her thoughts. "Gotta turn here."

It was faster for them to walk down Patsy's street and turn where it met Wedgewood School, but they almost never did because the Protestant kids would throw snowballs at them. The uniform was a dead giveaway. The kids at Wedgewood sometimes put stones inside the snowballs, or made them as icy as they could, so it really hurt if you got hit. But the Catholic kids did the same and were just as mean.

CHAPTER

2

Jules rushed out of school when the bell sounded. The sky was cloudy, and snow was sure to fall.

The Six Points Plaza wasn't on the way home, but it was one of the best places to be at Christmastime. There wasn't any other shopping center near her part of Etobicoke – except maybe the Cloverdale Mall, but people had to drive or take a bus to get there.

Part of the big parking lot in front of the plaza had been set up to sell Christmas trees. Jules loved to walk among the trees and imagine she was in a forest. They smelled wonderful. A huge wooden Santa with his sleigh and reindeer was perched on the plaza's flat roof. And in every store window, Christmas lights twinkled, showing off red, green, gold, and silver decorations.

Magical.

Jules walked quickly to Zellers and went inside. She could've stood at the entrance all afternoon, just looking at everything. But mean store clerks would nag her, asking, "Can I help you with something," when they knew damn well she couldn't buy anything.

First she looked at the decorations, then she went over to the candy counter and imagined which box of chocolate she'd buy, which candy canes, which candies. She was hungry, though, so she couldn't stay there for very long.

The next stop was the toy department. It didn't matter if it was supposed to be a boy's toy or a girl's, Jules loved them all and played with whatever she could.

She'd met two nice people who always worked in that department. A teenager, Frances, was usually there on Fridays and Saturdays or when the store was extra-busy. She was sixteen and went to Etobicoke Collegiate. She never acted stuck-up or mean.

Mrs. Adamson worked there all the time. She was about as old as most of the moms Jules knew. People might have said she was ordinary-looking because she didn't wear makeup or lipstick, like a lot of moms, or do anything with her dark shiny hair. But Jules didn't think her face was ordinary at all. Maybe it was because of her amazing smiles. They zapped you, making you feel good inside, forcing you to smile back.

Or maybe it was because of her big dark eyes, which seemed to see everything – not just the kids who wandered everywhere, touching and threatening to break the toys. She seemed to be able to tell what people were feeling the same way that other people noticed what you were wearing. More than once, she'd looked at Jules's face and said or done something to turn Jules's bad mood around.

Mrs. Adamson always gave Jules a person-to-person hello as Jules came in, and whenever the store wasn't busy, they'd talk. She figured out that Jules went to Our Lady of Peace, the only Catholic school around, from Jules's uniform. Mrs. Adamson's twin boys went there, too.

Jules told her she was in Grade 7, a grade ahead of some other kids her age, because she'd skipped a grade a couple of years before. It didn't mean she was smart, though. Her dad had said the principal was pushing many of the parents to let their kids jump a grade because too many students enrolled at the school the same time Jules did.

Jules had also told her she lived alone with her dad, not too far from the plaza. Mrs. Adamson didn't ask about her mom – probably because Jules never talked about her. She must have thought she was dead or something. Gone, anyway.

Mrs. Adamson didn't seem to mind that Jules never bought anything, and Jules was happy about that because this was the best place, the happiest place to be at Christmas.

Back when they lived closer to downtown, Jules and her father had once gone to see the Eaton's Santa

Claus Parade, and when it was over, they'd spent time looking at the "glorioso" window displays at Simpson's and Eaton's. They topped it all off with hotdogs and Orange Crush at the snack bar in Eaton's Annex. That was a never-to-be-forgotten day.

But Jules could feel the Christmas spirit at the plaza, and that's all that mattered. She stayed in Zellers as long as possible, playing lightly with as many toys as she could. The doll she wanted so badly was out of its box. Its beautiful red velvet dress was trimmed with lace. The doll's dark brown hair was long, with gorgeous curls. Jules loved to touch it and pull the long strands through her fingers. Gently, she took the doll down from the shelf.

Mrs. Adamson was watching her.

Jules looked back as if to ask her if it was okay to hold the doll, and Mrs. Adamson smiled, nodding yes.

Oh, how lovely, how perfect it is!

When Jules finally put the doll back on the shelf, she realized it was getting late. She'd have to get home.

On the way out of the toy department, Mrs. Adamson waved to her. "Bye. See you soon!"

And Jules felt happy.

She put her tuque and mitts back on, took a deep breath, and headed out into the growing darkness.

In front of the shops, it felt Christmassy — but things changed as soon as she left the plaza. Too many cars roared along the wide street she had to walk along, splattering mud and slush everywhere. Store owners often had going-out-of-business signs in their windows because people didn't want to shop there.

Jules always walked home on the side of the street that had the most houses. They were set back from the road as if they, too, wanted to get away from the traffic and car fumes.

It was five o'clock when she got home. Her dad was out. *Maybe he's gone to work after all.* He'd made a mess in the kitchen. She set her schoolbag down, cleaned off the kitchen table, and started to wash the dishes in the sink. She was hungry, hungry, hungry – hungrier than her dad most of the time. He never thought about food, and Jules always had to remind him they were running out.

She was almost afraid to open the fridge.

Okay. What do we have? The rotten milk I forgot to dump out. A jar of pickles. Shriveled-up celery with brown spots. Yucky Cheez Whiz. Ketchup. Now there's a meal!

She opened the cupboard and took down the last two cans of soup. Tomato. She poured both into a pot, added water, and heated it up on the stove. She used a mug to scoop the soup into a big bowl and added torn pieces of bread to thicken it. As carefully as she could, she carried the bowl to the living room and turned on the TV.

Please, let there be a Christmas program!

No luck. She turned the TV off and finished eating. After she washed the dishes, she pulled out

her recorder. In class they were learning how to play
Christmas songs for the school concert. Jules loved
her recorder and never got tired of practicing. She
had to play when her father wasn't around, though,
because the sound of it got on his nerves. Music
usually comforted her, but tonight she couldn't
remember the notes to some of the songs and kept
making mistakes.

It had been a hard-to-get-through day, for reasons
she couldn't explain to herself. Even though she'd
been happy in the department store, she felt more
lonely and sad now than she had in a long time. If
she let herself think about everything – without
imagining she was a princess, trapped, alone in a
castle, or an all-powerful superhero saving the world
– she might start to cry and never stop.

If her dad wasn't home by now, he wouldn't be
home at all – or at least not early enough to spend
time with her. Jules went to her room, turned on
the old lamp, and made her blanket fort. Her stomach
was full, and she'd be warm. That would help lift her
mind away.

CHAPTER

3

Jules leaned out of bed to look out the window at the morning sky. It was cloudy. Everything was gray and dull.

She didn't want to get out from under the blankets, but she also didn't want to miss school. Sometimes she'd forget to set her alarm, and rather than show up late, she'd just skip the whole day. Her dad almost never woke her up for school – he was either hung-over, sleeping most of the day, or had already gone to work.

It was okay to skip if the weather was warm. She could go to the park or just stay at home and watch TV. But in winter, the house never really got warm. Her dad turned down the furnace during the day, so that it was on just enough to keep the pipes from freezing. The cold made the house feel sad inside. Sometimes she'd go out and play in the snow, making a snow fort in the strip of backyard they had, but it was more fun to do that with friends.

The worst part of missing school was feeling so alone, like she was the only person left in the entire world. It was harder than being afraid of the dark or getting picked on by school bullies. Besides, as it got closer to Christmas, they spent lots of time in school preparing for the Christmas concert, making decorations, and reading Christmas stories – so most days were fun.

Her teacher, Mrs. Fournier, was reading *A Christmas Carol* to the class this week. And even though a lot of the kids didn't understand the weird English, they'd heard enough versions of the story to know what was going on.

Jules got ready and went downstairs. Her dad had made another mess in the kitchen, but at least he'd come home. She was glad of that. He was probably at work now.

She decided to walk to school by herself. She usually did her best imagining at night in her fort, but some days, especially raw angry days, she used her fantasies to make life different in the daytime, too. She'd pretend she was trekking through the desert or was a secret agent being followed by spies.

Jules saw Patsy just before reaching the school yard and caught up to her.

"Do you want to go skating after school?" Patsy asked. "Teresa's dad finished making the skating rink in their backyard."

Teresa's skating rink. Of all the great things in the world, that is one of the greatest.

Teresa's backyard bordered the park near Jules's place. She could even walk there with her skates on. "I sure do." Then she thought more about it. She wanted to invite Patsy over, but she'd left the house in a mess. And she'd have nothing to give her if she was hungry.

"I'll get home around three-thirty," Patsy said, "and can be at Teresa's about twenty minutes later. Meet me there? We'll have at least an hour to play."

"That's great," Jules said, relieved.

After school, Jules raced home. She took the stairs two at a time to go change.

Darn! No clean clothes!

She grabbed a pair of dirty jeans and a sweater from the floor, put them on, made a margarine sandwich, ate it fast, found her skates, and squeezed into them. They were getting too small; her toes were going to hurt something awful, but she didn't care.

When she got outside, the air was biting and a light snow was starting to fall. From the back gate of her house, looking across the park, she could see Teresa's yard.

As long as it doesn't snow too much, the rink'll be fine.

When she reached Teresa's, the rink was better than fine. It was big and wide, and the ice was pretty smooth.

Heaven!

She skated across it to the other side, crunched through the snow to Teresa's back door, and knocked.

Teresa was just inside, sitting on one of the stairs that led up to the kitchen. She already had a tuque on, and a thick sweater covered the top of her snow pants. Her skates were at the foot of the stairs.

"I'm almost ready, Jules. Gotta get my jacket and skates on. I'll be out in a sec."

Jules crunched back to the rink, raised her hands to the sky, and stuck her tongue out to catch falling snowflakes.

Hurray! My own private ice rink!

Carefully, because there were always a few bumps and cracks, she circled the rink, then skated to the center and spun around. She didn't know how to twirl like the ice skaters on TV, but she bet she could learn if someone taught her.

She began to skate faster and faster and faster, round and round the rink. The frosty air whipped by and felt great against her face. She hunched down as she moved, imagining she was a speed skater.

Teresa came out, and — from a distance — Jules could see Patsy coming down the street next to the park. Patsy was a strong skater, too. Teresa was no match for them, even though she had her own rink. But Teresa didn't seem to care, and why should she? They played all kinds of games, and you didn't have to be a fast skater to be good at them.

Later, a couple of kids from the neighborhood came over, and they all started to play ice tag.

Everyone shrieked and laughed as they tried to get away from the person who was "it." They bumped into each other and fell down. Or, even better, they fell when they were going really fast and skidded on their backsides across the ice into a snowbank.

Jules laughed until her stomach was sore. She didn't want the skating to end. But it got too dark, and they started bumping into each other – not even on purpose.

"Teresa! Teresa!" her mom called out. "Supper!"

Teresa told Jules and Patsy they could skate on the rink as long as they liked.

"I can't feel my toes, Jules," Patsy said when they were alone. "They're frozen. They're going to hurt like crazy when I get my skates off."

"Mine, too. But so what? We're tough, aren't we?"

"Tougher than tough."

"And fast."

"Faster than a speeding bullet!"

"Supermen!"

They raced each other around the rink for another fifteen minutes, pretending to be ice skaters in a competition.

"I don't want to go home, but I'd better before my toes fall off," Patsy finally said.

"Can't let that happen. I'll walk you to the end of the street."

They made their way through the small park. The road Patsy took to Teresa's was never plowed in winter. Snow got packed to the pavement by cars, and if the snow melted a bit and then the temperature dropped, the road became icy and easy to skate on.

They arrived at Bloor Street, said good-bye, and Jules retraced her steps, turning back through the park and into her own backyard.

A light shone from the kitchen window.

He's home!

Jules opened the back door quickly. "Hi, Dad!" She took her skates off in a minute. There was a lot of noise coming from the kitchen, which meant her father was cooking.

We're going to eat a regular meal. A perfect end to a perfect day!

"What're you making?"

"Spaghetti." He filled a pot with water for the noodles and gave the sauce a stir.

Jules got plates from the cupboard and set the table. "Do you think there's a Christmas program or movie on tonight we could watch together?"

"Dunno."

Jules's dad used to have the Christmas spirit long before the holiday arrived. He loved Christmas programs, Christmas songs on the radio, decorations, and lights – that's why Jules loved Christmas so much herself. But in the last couple of years, he'd changed. And Jules had to work really hard to get him in the mood.

"Are you going out tonight?"

"Nope. Maybe tomorrow. After I get home. After the shopping."

On Friday nights, her dad went to Loblaws at the Six Points Plaza.

"Do you want me to meet you at Loblaws? I can help."

"No. You'll just want me to buy all kinds of stuff."

"No, I won't. Honest. But you should see all the Christmas decorations in the stores. And there's all kinds of great toys and chocolate and candies in Zellers."

"Sounds as if someone's hungry."

Jules laughed. "I can hardly wait to eat."

He put the dried noodles in the boiling water. "Shouldn't be long now." He turned around to look at the table. "Pretty bare, huh? It'd be good if we could put cheese on this spaghetti or eat it with garlic bread."

"There's Cheez Whiz in the fridge, but it's kinda dried-up and old."

"Doesn't matter. We'll eat what we've got."

"Then maybe watch TV together?"

"Sure."

Jules didn't know how much boys ate, but she seemed to eat a lot for a girl − or so her dad said. But she just ate when she was hungry and until her stomach was full. Tonight she ate two plates of spaghetti. When they were finished, her dad went into the living room to watch the news while she did the dishes.

When she joined him, Jules kept her fingers crossed that there'd be something good on. "*Mr. Magoo's*

Christmas Carol's just starting. Want to watch it, Dad?"

"Sounds good."

Her father loved Mr. Magoo, but his "bumblingness" drove Jules crazy.

Doesn't matter. Just watching a Christmas show with him'll be fun.

Even before the program was over, Jules felt herself getting sleepy. She'd eaten so much spaghetti that her belly was bulging. The warm house and food made her warm inside, and she couldn't keep her eyes open.

"I'm going to bed, Dad."

"Okay."

"Have a good sleep."

"You, too."

When she got to her room, she changed quickly.

Yikes! It's like the North Pole up here.

She got into bed as fast as she could.

I won't be imagining anything tonight. I'm falling asleep standing up!

CHAPTER

4

The alarm clock rang. Another gray day outside.

Brrr. This room is freezing.

Jules got up and dressed quickly.

Friday the thirteenth. Yikes. But it's payday and Dad's going shopping. There'll be food in the fridge! And maybe he'll buy me a Christmas present.

It wasn't often Jules woke up feeling so good.

She washed her face and combed her straggly brown hair. Jules often wished it could be dark red or black – something dramatic. She went downstairs to the kitchen. Her dad was already gone.

No milk. No bread, even. How am I going to make breakfast? Or lunch?

She heated up the leftover spaghetti on the stove. If she ate a big enough breakfast, it wouldn't be so hard to miss lunch. She filled her stomach as much as she could bear, cleaned up the kitchen, and got ready for school.

She was going to walk with Patsy today. They'd plan the weekend. Maybe they'd go skating at Teresa's again or, even better, go to the plaza and play "Pretend" – pretend to buy this or that, pretend to be this or that person.

Patsy was slow getting ready, and they had to run most of the way to school, which was hard to do because the sidewalks were slippery. It was fun, though – the funnest part of the day.

At lunch, despite the big spaghetti breakfast, Jules was hungry all over again, but she had to pretend she wasn't. She went outside and watched some of the kids go home, the ones who lived nearby.

Will their mom or dad be there? Will there be food in the fridge or cupboards? Will they make the same kind of meal I do?

It was hard to keep warm, just standing and waiting, and it seemed a long time before the rest of the kids came outside. Some were holding cookies or an apple or orange. Jules watched them eat and imagined the taste of the food in her own mouth. She couldn't help it.

Tonight Dad goes shopping, and maybe he'll buy a treat.

That thought made her happy.

After school, Jules got to Zellers in record time. She bypassed the candy section – her stomach was too growly – and went straight for the dolls. Hers was still on display, which meant she could play with it.

She'd told her dad the name of the doll she wanted way back in October, and over and over again since then. She'd told him the price, too.

I hope he remembers. I don't want anything else for Christmas.

"You're getting too old to play with dolls, aren't you?" he'd said last week.

"No, I'm not, Dad. Lots of my friends still do."

He looked like he didn't believe her, but she didn't know how to convince him. She'd thought about asking for something else, a book maybe. She loved to read.

But once you're finished a book, that's it. With a doll, you can play and play and play. It becomes a friend. Something to love.

Mrs. Adamson came over to where Jules was standing. "Hi, Jules. How're you doing?"

"Okay." Jules smiled shyly.

"You love that doll, don't you?"

Jules nodded.

"I wish I'd had one like it when I was small."

"Really?" Jules looked at the expression on Mrs. Adamson's face to see if she was being phony.

"The few I did get I managed to keep, though. I still love them."

Jules wanted to say that she'd kept her dolls from many years ago, too – but she had only a couple left, and they were in pretty bad shape. When she was little, she liked to experiment with their hair and try to figure out how the leg and arm joints worked by pulling them off. Or she'd make the dolls go on wild outdoor adventures they often didn't survive. But she wasn't like that now.

I'm going to take care of this one if I get it. And I'll take it with me if we move again. I've lost too much.

Mrs. Adamson talked to her a lot that day, in between customers. It was hard to know what to say back, but that didn't seem to bother Mrs. Adamson. She talked about any darn thing, and she answered Jules as if she was really listening.

"It's great working in the toy department because I can get lots of bargains. I love toys almost as much as my kids do."

When Mrs. Adamson went over to rearrange a display some customers had messed up, Jules watched her and wondered why some adults treated kids as if they didn't remember being one, and others treated kids as if they never forgot.

CHAPTER

5

Jules got home around five o'clock, tidied up, and played her recorder.

An hour later, the usual worries began.

"What's keeping him?" she said out loud.

It isn't snowing. That can't be it.

He has to work overtime. That happens sometimes.

There's an extra-long lineup at the bank. Fridays are busy.

Crowds in the supermarket. For sure.

Not many taxis. Not at this time of night.

All those things.

But when her dad was late, it was almost always because he went for a few beers with his work buddies and forgot the time, especially on payday.

By seven-thirty, Jules had just about given up when she heard her dad fumbling with the outer screen door.

"Jules, Jules, I need your help," he called out. Taxi drivers often helped him carry the groceries in, but not today. He took a taxi home on Fridays because he had so much to carry, but also because he smashed up their old wreck of a car a year ago, along with somebody else's. That was scary. He almost went to jail.

Jules didn't care if they had a car, although her dad was an auto mechanic, and he thought it was crazy that they couldn't afford to buy one. He worked at Thompson Motors and could make any kind of rotten car go.

"Hi, Dad. I'll take the bags."

"Hi, honey!" he said in a loud voice.

His whole body smells of beer.

"I was getting worried about you."

"What the hell for? I made pretty good time, pretty good time."

"Sure. It's not so late." Jules carried the groceries to the kitchen table and went through the bags eagerly to see what was in them.

On days when her dad drank a lot, he bought things he wouldn't normally get, like fancy cuts of meat or canned asparagus, forgetting to buy milk or bread. But it looked as though he'd covered the basics and bought only a few weird extras.

"How often do we have steak, Jules? We're going to have steak tonight. Steak and potatoes and mushrooms."

"Did you buy potatoes, Dad? We're all out."

"Sure, I think I did." He started searching through the bags. "Whoops," he said, laughing like a little boy. "Guess I forgot. But it's okay. I got some fantastic bread. We'll have that and steak and mushrooms, and I even bought dessert." He pulled out a package of brownies and a box of powdered strawberry doughnuts.

Jules's eyes lit up. "Great. I can hardly wait."

"You're a poet and don't know it."

They both laughed.

She put the groceries away while he cooked. Before long, dinner was ready. Jules didn't like steak as much as her father, but she'd eat anything.

He kept drinking.

"I'm finished, Dad. Can I have dessert?"

"Sure, hon."

Powdered strawberry doughnuts. Ooey-gooey good!

She gobbled one down.

Her dad was in a good mood, but she knew from experience that beer was more responsible for it than the fact that it was payday and Friday night. It didn't matter, though.

After she'd done the dishes, they turned on the TV. Jules hoped her dad would just get tired and fall asleep.

She looked outside the living room window. It had started to snow. She asked if she could have some of the canned orange drink he'd bought.

"Okay, but that's got to last. I don't want it all gone tonight."

"No, no. I won't drink it all." But she could have. It tasted so good, and she never seemed to get enough.

She gulped the orange drink quickly and went back to the living room. Her father was having another beer. She'd counted the empty bottles when she was in the kitchen, like she always did.

"Just a lot of crap!" he said, switching channels.

Jules could stay up late any night of the week when her dad wasn't around, but if he was, he let her stay up as long as she wanted on Friday and Saturday nights. If she'd been playing hard outside during the day, she usually got sleepy by eight o'clock.

She wasn't tired tonight, though. And she was still hungry. "Dad, can I have a brownie?"

"Goddamn it! Are you going to eat everything?"

"No! I won't, I won't. It's just that I'm still kinda hungry."

"Hungry? After all I made for you? After all you ate? Goddamn it. Goddamn *you*!" He stormed into the kitchen.

Jules thought about making a run for her room, but hiding wasn't always the best thing to do when her dad wanted to yell at her. He'd get angry if she bolted, and he'd chase her, screaming and yelling outside her locked bedroom door, making her feel trapped. Sometimes if she just stayed put, shrinking herself down and pretending she wasn't there, things would calm down.

"Here!" He threw the cardboard package of

brownies at her, hitting her on her cheek. "Eat them! Eat them all!" He thundered into the kitchen again and came back carrying the can of orange drink and the doughnuts. "Here, finish all this off, too!" He slammed the doughnuts and drink down on the floor in the middle of the living room and stomped back into the kitchen. "I work hard all day at a job I hate. Spend all my money on groceries, and she wants to eat everything in one night! All right! Okay! Then that's what she's gonna do. Here!" he roared as he brought out a bag of carrots, a package of bologna, a loaf of bread, eggs.

He kept going back and forth from the kitchen to the living room, taking whatever he could find from the fridge and cupboards, and putting the food in the middle of the living room floor. "Go on. Eat it! Finish it all, like the goddamn pig you are! And when there's nothing left, it ain't gonna be my fault."

Jules bent her head down into her chest. Her dad never liked it if she looked straight at him when he was like this.

He marched back to the kitchen. Jules knew what people meant when they said someone was larger than life. Her dad looked and acted like a giant, a giant on a rampage. He was banging the cupboard doors as he opened and closed them, screaming and grabbing more food.

Time to escape.

Jules hadn't seen him this crazy for a long time.

What if he forces me to eat the food he's piling up?

That thought was terrifying. If she was fast enough, she could get upstairs before he noticed. If he followed her to her room, she could lock the door. She put the brownies on the sofa and ran.

When she got to her room, Jules locked herself in and listened at the door. It was important to know what was going on, though, so she decided to open the door a few inches in order to hear him.

When he realized she wasn't there, the rampaging got worse. He threw dishes on the kitchen floor and against the walls. Smashing stuff was one of his favorite things to do when he got mad – or destroying something Jules cared about.

"What does she expect? Goddamn kid! I've had it. I'm done!" Then she heard him dialing a number on the phone. His voice changed to the one he used for his friends. "Hey, Hank. Yeah, it's me. Got anything going on tonight? Wanna go to the Izzy?"

There was a silence as Hank answered.

"Great! Get yourself over here and let's do it. It's Chrismus, for Chrissake. I wanna have some fun."

As her father listened to Hank, it felt as if the house itself were catching its breath.

"Yeah? Perfect. I'm ready." He slammed the receiver down.

He'd once pulled the phone wire out of the wall and thrown the entire set across the living room. But then they couldn't use the phone for a long time.

"A goddamn leech, a bloody stinking leech, that's

what she is!" His voice got louder, stronger, rising out of his chest like a lion's roar. It could take over a room and squeeze out every other sound. "I'm stuck. Stuck in this stupid life! I work hard and come home to 'gimme, gimme, gimme.' Christ! I can't take it!"

He kept shouting and smashing things, even though she wasn't downstairs. He did it because they were the only two people left in the world.

When Hank's car pulled up, Jules heard one final crash. Then the front door slammed, and he was gone.

She'd been too afraid to cry before, but the tears came now, without a sound. She'd learned to cry like that. If her dad suddenly came back, the sound of her could set him off again.

When she tripped or fell or got hurt or was slapped, she felt pain and cried, but the pain she felt now was different.

She'd have to make things right – clean everything up and pretend it hadn't happened. She'd have to try and watch her dad better. She should have known tonight might be one of his bad nights because of all the drinking. But it was so hard to tell – he sometimes laughed and looked happy just before he exploded.

One good thing was that she didn't have to do silent crying for long. She heard Hank's old car drive away. Now she could add sound to the tears, like she needed to. That would help get some of the hurt out of her body.

Jules went downstairs and into the living room. Her dad had thrown one of their old wooden chairs against the wall and a leg had broken off. And he'd kicked the can of orange drink, splattering the liquid onto the sofa and wall behind it. The smelly brown carpet was wet in places, too.

She went into the kitchen. Her father had broken a few glasses and plates. She dreaded cleaning them up. It was hard to get all the pieces because there were so many splinters you couldn't see.

She got some toilet paper to blow her nose, sat down on the floor in the kitchen doorway, and started rocking herself back and forth. Tears rolled down her cheeks, and from the back of her throat came the hard dry sound of her cries. Her thin body shook as she tried to push the awfulness out.

If she could take her mind away from what had happened, she'd feel better. But it felt as if she were crumbling into a thousand pieces. It was hard to find the part of her that felt normal, breathing-in-and-out normal. The pain inside made it difficult to move.

She forced herself to get up, clean the kitchen, and carry everything from the living room back to the refrigerator and cupboards. It took a long time because she wasn't Jules the person anymore; she was all used up.

She looked at the brownies and doughnuts. She couldn't eat them now, even if they were rammed down her throat.

If I get up before my dad tomorrow, if he sleeps late, if he doesn't come home — if, if, if! — I'll have time to wash the drink off everything and put the living room back in order.

She dragged herself upstairs and changed. She couldn't feel anything, even the iciness of the room or the beauty of the snowy night outside her window. She lay in bed, staring at nothing.

CHAPTER

6

It was early morning when Jules woke up and tiptoed into her father's room. His bed hadn't been slept in. No surprise there. He often stayed out with his buddies all night on a Friday or Saturday.

Jules breathed a sigh of relief.

At least I won't be here when he comes home.

She went downstairs and took another look at the mess. Jules didn't know how she was going to make the orange drink stains go away, but she filled a bucket with soapy water and scrubbed to make everything less sticky. When she was finished and looked at what she'd done, it seemed as if she'd made an even bigger mess — but that wasn't really true. Once everything dried, it would look the same as before. That's what she hoped.

Gotta get back to normal. Gotta make things right.

Yesterday, she'd looked forward to having milk

with her cereal, but her appetite was gone. She knew
she should eat, though, because she intended to stay
out all day, until it got dark.

She ate a bit of cereal, cleared up, and got dressed
– putting on extra layers. She might have to wander
around outside for a long time.

Being Saturday, Patsy would be home and want
to play. But Jules couldn't see her. Not yet.

Jules would go to the plaza. She'd watch people
buy Christmas trees or go in and out of the stores,
pretending she was like anyone else.

Outside was a winter wonderland. Six inches of
new snow. The sun was shining, and the sky was
blue. She got to Zellers around noon. Mrs. Adamson
was there. Jules kept her head down as she walked
into the toy department. She didn't want Mrs.
Adamson to notice she wasn't herself.

Despite everything that had happened, it felt so
good to see the doll. It was strange how something
beautiful could make you feel good inside.

Jules played with it as long as she could, but it was
still too early to go home. She headed to the
storybook section. Mrs. Adamson was watching her
again.

Great. Maybe she even thinks I'll steal something!

But, no. Mrs. Adamson caught Jules's gaze, smiled,
and nodded. There were no customers around.

"Hi there," she said, coming over to Jules.

"Hi."

"What happened to your cheek?"

"Snowball."

"Oh." Mrs. Adamson looked at her steadily.

Jules had been at the store until dark on Friday, long past the time for snowball fights. If she'd been hit by one Saturday morning, her cheek would be redder, not turning black and blue.

"Um, why don't you sit down there, Jules, where there's a clear spot on the lower shelf? It'll be more comfortable to read."

Jules was on the verge of crying and couldn't say thanks. There was a worried look in Mrs. Adamson's eyes.

Jules grabbed a book quickly so she could put her face down.

A baby's book! A first reader. Borrring!

When Frances called Mrs. Adamson to help her, Jules pretended to look at the pictures until the urge to cry was over. As she was able to relax, she looked for something better. She'd read most of the fairy tales that were there. Many of the kids' books were too corny, too cute. Jules loved using her imagination, but stories for kids her age often didn't have much imagination at all. The best stories make a person feel as if they are part of a completely different world.

Even if it's a down-on-earth one. That's what I do when I imagine.

She picked up another book and another, finally settling on a comic. *Superman* was one of the best. It'd be wonderful to be Superman. She often dreamt about it.

She looked up at the big clock on the wall near the store entrance. Three o'clock.

I'll just take my time going home. Play outside in the snow first. Dad should be there and feeling okay by then.

She felt grateful to Mrs. Adamson for the way she'd treated her.

Jules got to her place by going the back way through the park. No lights shone from the windows. It was going to be hard to be in that old house alone. She looked out over the park. In the distance, she could see kids skating on Teresa's rink.

Funny how hard it is to do anything when you're feeling sad inside.

Jules didn't want anyone to see her, and she didn't have the heart to make castle rooms in the snow.

Her stomach was growling. Now would be a good time to eat, even if her dad did come home and make dinner – she wouldn't need much and he wouldn't get angry.

Jules opened the fridge.

At least there's food to eat.

She made herself a bologna and cheese sandwich. No orange drink.

Oh, well. There's milk.

She carried her dinner to the living room and turned on the TV. Saturday afternoon at four-thirty had to be the worst possible time for watching television.

Nothing on. Nothing!

So she watched nothing. When she was finished eating, she took her plate to the kitchen, tidied up, and went back to the TV.

Please! Something about Christmas!

"Lawrence Welk."

Oh, brother!

Her dad hated that show because it was so corny. But *she* watched it. People sang Christmas carols and looked happy.

She managed to forget the time. About ten o'clock, she decided to go to bed.

Tonight I'll use my imagination. Much better than TV.

She built her cozy fort in her room and closed her eyes.

CHAPTER

7

S unday morning.

Dad must've come home late, if he came home at all. I was awake for a long time but didn't hear him come in.

Jules went to his room.

Still gone.

She didn't know the telephone numbers for his friends. Didn't know what she'd ask them if she could phone.

Dad would get mad at me.

Her grandma was thousands of miles away in Vancouver, and Jules had met her only twice in her life. That had been enough. And there was no one else.

She started to think back over the last few months. Her dad had been drinking a lot more and was unhappy most of the time. She always tried to push those thoughts away to another part of her brain and pretend that things were okay. She had to shove the scary thoughts out or she'd explode.

He's been away before, weeknights or whole weekends. This is no different.

She went back to her bedroom and looked out the window for a long, long time. Houses ran along either side of the small park. They were all the same size and shape, even though each family tried to make theirs look unique by painting the outside a different color, adding shutters to the windows, or growing unusual plants and shrubs in the small gardens. Each yard was about the same size. In summer, the street became a stamp collection of green lawns. Jules always thought everything looked much more beautiful in winter, even though the snow covered the yards in the same way. It didn't make sense, but maybe the ugly sameness of every-thing wasn't as obvious.

The sky was always changing, though. In winter, the only skies she hated were the gray, gloomy ones, when it didn't snow and the sun didn't come out and the whole world looked sad.

She went downstairs to the kitchen. She wasn't hungry, but her dad would probably get mad if the food he'd bought wasn't being eaten. She just didn't have much of an appetite anymore.

She ate a small bowl of cereal and didn't bother to clean up.

I'll have to push myself outside today.

It seemed to take forever to put on the extra layer of clothes she'd need to keep warm. She kept forgetting something, but finally went outside.

The blast of icy air that hit her was a shock. Jules didn't think she'd be able to feel anything.

Okay, okay. What'll I do? Where'll I go? No stores open. Damn!

She decided to walk up to Wedgewood School. There was an outdoor skating rink beside it, an official one that was looked after by the city. She wouldn't take her skates, but there'd be skaters and she could watch them. If kids from school were there, they'd be playing hockey, break the whip, or ice tag.

She wanted to stretch out the time it took to get there. She couldn't go up Martin Grove – it would have gotten her there faster, but she couldn't risk meeting Patsy or someone from Patsy's family. She had to walk farther along Bloor and cut across Charleston, the street where Jerry Chambers lived. He was a mean, ugly kid who acted like a big shot. If she bumped into him, he'd make her feel worse than she already did – but that was a chance she'd have to take.

She could hear the sound of skaters' voices before she got to the rink. It was Sunday, so moms and dads were with their kids. Bullies don't push, trip, or chase anybody when parents are around. She should've remembered that.

Jules stood behind the boards surrounding the rink. She watched as a young couple put skates on their little boy as fast as they could, to prevent his little feet from freezing.

When his skates were done up, he held on to his parents' hands and tried to walk on the ice as if he had shoes on, not skates. That was funny. His upper body couldn't catch up with his feet, and he fell on his behind. He started to cry, but Jules could tell he was just surprised, not hurt.

"It's okay, honey. You're all right, sweetheart," his mom said. "You have to go like this. Here, watch how Mommy's doing it. Take tiny, tiny steps, let the blade of the skate stay down on the ice, and push a little. It'll move you ahead."

He tried over and over again but kept falling — although he expected it now.

Eventually, the mother took one arm, the father the other, and the boy was able to stay upright. Sometimes the parents held him up so high that it looked as if he were flying and dancing in the air. When that happened, he squealed with joy.

Jules tried to remember when she'd learned to skate. Her father used to be a good hockey player, so he must have taught her. But maybe her mother, Celia, was the one. She hadn't left them until Jules was four.

Jules didn't have any pictures of her. Her dad had ripped them up and thrown away the pieces. He never wanted to talk about her. But as Jules got older, she wanted, needed, to have an image of her mom in her head.

She'd ask about her only when her dad was in a

good mood. "Did she look like me?"

"Yeah. Your hair exactly. Your nose, mouth."

"Was she pretty?"

"What a question. Yes, Jules."

"Where'd she grow up? In Toronto, like us?"

"No. Georgetown."

"Is that far?"

"Not really."

"What about her family, her mom and dad? Are they here?"

"Her mom and dad lived on a farm. Don't know where they are now. Don't care."

"How'd you meet my . . . mom?" The last word was hard to get out.

"At the Palais."

"What's the Palais?"

"A dance hall. Celia loved to dance."

"Was she a good dancer?"

"Good enough. We both were."

Jules wanted to believe that her mother meant more to her father than the other girlfriends he'd had. Seeing how sore his heart was, maybe she had.

If he stayed in a good mood, he'd usually give her a hug and tell her how much he loved her. "Enough with the questions, kiddo," he'd say. "We don't need anybody else hanging around us, do we? We've got each other. That's all that matters."

One of the girls from her class called out to Jules from the other side of the rink. Jules pretended she couldn't hear her and began walking home.

Ai yai yai. I wonder what the temperature is? Teresa's rink'll be even better than it was before. And skating'll make me warm. Anything's better than standing around.

She took the long way home again, to avoid Patsy's place, and went through the park. Kids were skating on Teresa's rink, but Jules changed her mind about going there. She couldn't bring herself to join them.

Opening the back door of the house, she tried to make as much noise as she could, banging her feet against the stairs. There were no other sounds but hers.

She sat just inside the door to get warm for a bit, then went outside again. With all the new snow, it'd be a good day to convert the backyard into a castle, with throne rooms and dungeons. She and Patsy loved to pretend they were powerful Gypsy queens, wild and free, who lived in snow castles. It would be a lot of work clearing the space, making barricades for the castle front, and gathering mounds of snow for the thrones. But it would keep her warm, and, being near the house, she'd know when her dad got back.

When night came, she looked up at the stars and all around at the white night of snow. It looked like a painting.

A painting that's getting colder and colder to be inside. Have to go in.

It had felt like a never-ending day. But there was school tomorrow. It would take her mind off things.

I'll eat and watch TV. Make my fort and send my mind somewhere else. What more can I do?

CHAPTER
8

Once inside the back door, Jules pulled off her outdoor clothes, threw them on the stairs, and stomped over them on her way up to the kitchen.

She wasn't really hungry, but she heated up a can of soup, made another bologna sandwich, and carried the food to the living room.

She ate slowly as she watched TV. After a while, the soup got cold.

"No, no, no . . ." Jules pushed her food away and began moaning.

He's not coming home tonight, either, and it's Sunday already.

She looked out the living room window and down the street, allowing herself to cry. The sounds she made got mixed in with the happy sounds of the Walt Disney program.

Nothing can touch me.

When she was all cried out, she went to the kitchen, washed the dishes, and cleaned up.

Make it clean, make it good, make him happy.

She headed upstairs and put on her pajamas.

I could stay up all night or run around outside if I wanted to – and he wouldn't know anything about it. Look at me. I can take care of myself.

She had trouble making the fort in her room because she didn't have any patience. It kept falling down.

Can nothing go right? These stupid blankets won't stay up!

Finally the fort held and she crawled in. For the longest time, all she could do was stare angrily at the pattern on the old blanket stretched out above her. The real world was awful, messy, hurting. When she got older, she'd find out about other worlds – or at least other ways to live. It couldn't be true that this was how life was supposed to be.

She'd try to imagine being Superman tonight. He was stronger than anybody, could do amazing feats, and travel anywhere he wanted in the blink of an eye. He was a man, but Jules didn't even think of that when she imagined herself as a superhero. It wasn't important. Girls imagined themselves as heroes – the male or female ones they read about or saw on TV or in the movies. Girls were courageous and strong in their minds despite how they were supposed to be.

She could fly and fly and fly – all over the planet –

or go to other planets, undiscovered, unexplored. Nothing was impossible. Demolishing buildings, moving mountains, throwing bombs into outer space, catching bullets.

Superman had weaknesses for sure, like Kryptonite, but usually he could get out of dangerous predicaments with the help of other superheroes or friends. She wasn't going to be a superhero who always had problems.

What's the point of being a superhero if you've got as many problems as a human? Or your superpowers are limited, and you have to fight villains with only ice or fire? Pathetic. As for Batman, he just uses fancy gadgets. And some of them are pretty dumb. When you get right down to it, there isn't anything superhero about him. He's boring. The person on top of the superhero totem pole is Superman.

That's the best thing about using your imagination. You can be exactly what you want.

Dammit. What's the point? Getting carried away by fantasies. Even believing in them. Like the one about Santa Claus. Everyone acts like he's real. Why do they do that when he isn't?

The idea that a magical figure like Santa exists makes people feel good inside. Makes them think that magical people and worlds are possible, that there could still be something good and beautiful and different under the ordinary surface of everything.

To be loved, to be happy, to be cared for, nourished body and soul. These things were never granted to shadows. And that's what she was – a shadow being.

There were others like her. But they couldn't help each other, couldn't be together. No one else could see her. Maybe that would be true for all time.

Shadows could look into the houses they passed. Could look into the lives of the people in them. Sometimes the families inside were happy, sometimes not.

When she saw children who were being slapped around, ignored, not cared for, hurt in different ways, she wanted to make things better.

But she couldn't. Shadows couldn't.

It was hard to see children being treated badly, but it was harder to watch children who were happy, playing with their brothers and sisters and friends, their parents near. That made her angry, filled her with despair.

There was nothing more terrible than being outside of everything, without enough of what you needed to live. That's how it was for Jules.

Why?

Maybe if she went deep enough into her pain, she'd find an answer. Children weren't meant to suffer in the way she suffered. She felt that much, knew that much.

Shadows can't exist without light. They are supposed to be together. She had to figure out why she was in this terrible world, what had made her a shadow.

She had to go back and back and back.

———

Jules opened her eyes. Total darkness. Something was covering her face, but she couldn't move. Her whole body was frozen, and she screamed in terror.

With sheer force of will, she sat up, pushing the heavy cloth away. She managed to stand, desperate to free herself from the blackness.

Am I in a nightmare, thinking I'm awake when I'm not? But if I'm awake, where am I?

Her heart pounded in her chest as the seconds passed.

Help me! Help me!

She held out her arms to see if anything was there.

Empty space.

She stepped forward and knocked something over. The sound terrified her until she realized what it was.

A lamp. A bedroom lamp.

She was in her own room. As her eyes finally adjusted, she could make out the door and walls, the window.

She could have cried out with relief, but the agony of the dream wouldn't leave her.

She went over to the window and knelt by it. The night was so dark. Her heart raced. She got the covers from the bed and wrapped them around her body. She could never go back to sleep.

CHAPTER
9

December 16. Morning. Another sunny day.
How can it be?
Jules lay on her bed, exhausted. It took a long time to find the energy to wash and change. She didn't feel like herself.

When she got down to the kitchen, she could see that nothing was different from the day before. The clock on the wall said eight o'clock.

I'm going to be late for school!

Jules quickly made two bologna sandwiches. No time for breakfast.

Better not eat too much. The food'll run out.

She ran-walked along the slippery, snow-packed sidewalks.

No long cuts today.

Jules got to school just as the bell rang. Her mind wasn't on schoolwork, and she didn't answer when

Mrs. Fournier asked her a question during math class.

"Stop daydreaming, Jules Doherty. I know there are only a few more days of school before Christmas, but you need to pay attention." Mrs. Fournier sounded fed up. "You're all driving me crazy!"

Mrs. Fournier wasn't mean, but she was pretty strict. Maybe she had to be. A bunch of kids had come into her Grade 7 class after skipping Grade 6. They bugged her all the time with questions.

At lunch, Patsy acted extra-goofy because she could tell Jules wasn't herself. Patsy was no fool.

The afternoon went by in a blur. Jules had already decided to go to the plaza after school, but she walked Patsy home first.

"See ya tomorrow," Patsy said. "I'll ask Mom if you can come over. Rosey won't be around to stick her nose up at whatever we do."

"Sure," Jules said absentmindedly.

When she got to the plaza, it was hard to look at the Christmas trees, the decorations, the people in the stores. Jules headed straight for Zellers and the toy department.

My doll.

She greeted it like a friend. It had a warm bright smile and a friendly look on its face. She glanced at other toys and dolls as well, but mostly she stayed with her doll.

Jules didn't want to go home, but eventually six o'clock came. Mrs. Adamson said good-bye, and Jules could feel her eyes on her back as she left the store.

"Yup, there goes Jules the weirdo," she's thinking. "Always here. Always by herself."

Outside, the temperature was falling. A harsh wind cut right through her. When she got to her street, she couldn't bring herself to look up at their house.

She tried to think what her father meant by staying away. He must have been so angry with her that he didn't want to see her. Ever. She knew she wasn't a good kid, but her father was happy to be with her some of the time.

Maybe he's hurt himself or been in an accident.

But someone would come tell me. The police or somebody from the hospital.

But if he's alone and unconscious, no one would know.

Jules went over and over the possibilities in her head. She always ended up back at zero, alone in that house and the whole world not seeing, not knowing.

Argh. My thoughts are driving me crazy. Have to push them away. Have to get inside the stupid house. Act normal. Eat dinner. Forget.

One of her dad's favorite meals was pork and beans on toast. So that's what she ate for dinner as she watched TV.

It was hard to pay attention, but Christmas was getting closer, so there were more and more TV programs, commercials, and movies about the holidays. She started to watch a movie about a family with a beautiful mother and father and a beautiful house surrounded by beautiful everything.

Is that how most people live?

No.

Patsy's family wasn't like that. Her mom and dad were poor and worked all the time, which is why Patsy and her sister had to babysit after school, on holidays, and almost every day in the summer. Lots of parents had to be away from home and had money problems, just like her dad.

She turned off the TV.

I'm not going to wash the stupid dishes, clean the house, or do anything. He can just come home and see a big mess for all I care!

Jules stomped up the stairs. She glanced into her dad's room before going into her own.

She made her blanket fort, but she felt suffocated inside it. Try as she might, she couldn't imagine anything. She took it down, got under the covers, and stared angrily at the ceiling.

Sleep wouldn't come.

She sat up, wrapped a blanket around herself, and went to the window to look out. As she knelt in front of the icy window, she could see her breath as she exhaled.

There were stars in the night sky, and the snowy world was a radiant white in the darkness. It didn't look real.

I don't feel like I'm in it, maybe that's why. I don't even feel like I'm here.

———

Jules woke up hopeful. She tiptoed into the hallway to look into her dad's room.

Empty. He's left me now. Until forever.

She stomped her feelings down. It was a school day, and she had to be there. School was part of the normal world, and she needed something normal to keep her from feeling like she didn't exist.

Jules wandered around the house and somehow managed to get dressed and out the door. She went up Martin Grove, hoping that Patsy hadn't left for school yet. She needed to talk to another human being. Luckily, Patsy was home.

"You're early, Jules," Mrs. O'Connor said, looking at the clock.

"Uh, yeah. I got ready really fast today."

"C'mon in. Patsy's still eating."

Patsy's house was full of noise. Everybody seemed to be talking and yelling at the same time from every room. Patsy was alone in the kitchen, stuffing cereal into her mouth, spilling drops of milk all over herself.

"Hey, Jules," she said, her cheeks bulging. "Glad you came over. Do you wanna go by Wedgewood School and shoot snowballs at the Protestant kids?"

"Sure."

Anything for a distraction.

"What's that you're going to do?" Mr. O'Connor asked as he walked into the kitchen.

"Oh, nothing, Dad."

"I don't want you coming home with another black eye."

Patsy beamed. She'd given as good as she got that day.

Jumping up from her place at the table, she said, "Let's get out of here, Jules. Or we'll have to go to school with my brother and sister." Patsy grabbed her coat and had it half on by the time she opened the back door. "Isn't this the ugliest coat you've ever seen on the face of the earth?"

"Gee, I don't know, Patsy. It's not that bad."

"I can hardly wait to grow out of it."

"But then you'll just get another of your sister's old jackets."

"She's not growing as fast as I am, Mom said. Maybe I'll get a new one next time. Yowee, it sure is freezing today!"

They had a wild snowball fight when they reached Wedgewood. Jules got hit in the face again. Same spot. Her cheek stung something awful.

Penance for a lie.

When they got to Mattice Avenue, the road the school was on, they ran. The bell would ring any minute.

Jules was glad she'd gone to school with Patsy. She felt almost normal.

There's no way I'm gonna go home after school, Jules told herself. She walked up to Bloor and over to the plaza instead.

Shoppers, lights, decorations — just the same old lousy Christmas stuff.

She went into Zellers, feeling embarrassed. Mrs. Adamson kept looking over at her. She tried playing with the toys and games in spots where Mrs. Adamson couldn't see her. But it was hard to do anything at all. Her heart wasn't into being there.

She headed over to her doll. Seeing it felt good for a few moments. She stood there staring at it, and she felt her mind slowly leave her body. Not in the good way it usually did when she was imagining things, but in the vanishing way she'd felt last night.

"That would be a wonderful Christmas present, wouldn't it?"

Jules almost jumped out of her skin. Mrs. Adamson was standing right beside her. Jules didn't want to give a friendly answer back.

"Yeah," she said quietly. Jules quickly turned away, but she knew Mrs. Adamson was still watching her. She stomped over to the empty spot at the book display and crashed down onto it.

I could break this whole stupid thing with a few kicks. Smash it all to pieces!

She was angry, so angry.

If I looked in a mirror right this second, I'd have the same kind of expression on my face as Dad's stupid friend Hank. He always looks angry and miserable.

Argh! Can't scream or they'll think I'm crazy.

Jules grabbed the first book beside her. Hans Christian Andersen.

No, thank you!

She turned to the other side of the display and reached over for a "real" book, a thick one.

I'll show her. I'll sit here and read as long as I want.

But . . . Mrs. Adamson won't mind. She never does.

Jules buried herself in the book. Two hours later, she heard the announcement telling shoppers that the store was closing.

Shoot! Gotta go to my stinking home.

Jules left the store before Mrs. Adamson could say one more kind thing to her.

When she got home, the house was dark.

CHAPTER

10

December 18. Wednesday.

Jules usually crossed off each day on the kitchen calendar, but she'd stopped doing it since Friday.

Doesn't matter anymore, does it?

The eighteenth meant something, though. She tried to think what.

Oh, yeah. The Christmas concert. The stupid Christmas concert. How am I going to go? I can't go alone – it finishes too late.

Last year, she and her dad had walked together to school, and it'd been fun.

Who wants to see me in the stupid concert anyway? I'll just pretend I'm going, pretend my dad's coming.

She stomped around the house.

I hate you, house, as much as you hate me! Stupid walls. Stupid brown carpet. Smelly, old kitchen. I hate you!

Jules started to cry.

She pushed herself outside, avoided Patsy's place, and kept her head down as she kicked through the snow. Eventually, she got to the outer limit of the school property.

I'm breaking apart.

Jules wondered if she could even get herself into the schoolyard. She tried to make her face look normal and joined some other kids who were having a snowball fight.

None of the kids in her class looked at her as if anything was wrong.

"Make sure you get here by six-thirty tonight," Mrs. Fournier said before dismissing the class. "And remember: clean uniforms. With cleaned and pressed shirt or blouse."

Jules felt a moment of panic. She had only one blouse, and it had stopped being clean or white a long time ago. Then she remembered she wasn't even going to the concert — and relief turned to sadness.

She left school without speaking to anyone and trudged through the snow in the direction of the plaza. It was getting harder to be there — to be anywhere without feeling like a lonely nothing, but she couldn't go home.

Oh, Dad. I'm sorry. I won't do it again. I won't ask for anything. I'll leave you alone. Just come back. Please!

She walked listlessly over to the Christmas trees in the plaza parking lot. Not many left. Christmas was only seven days away.

In Zellers, Mrs. Adamson was busy with a customer, and Frances was buzzing back and forth from the storeroom. The next couple of days would be hectic.

Why don't I give my doll a name? That'd be a good idea, even if I don't get her for Christmas. Let's see. Teresa, Terry, Elizabeth, Lizzie, Margaret, Maggie. Perfect! I call thee Maggie. And so it shall be for all time!

Jules smiled a real smile for the first time that day.

She wandered over to where the doll clothes were on display and pretended she had lots of money and could spend all of it on a complete wardrobe for Maggie. Out of the corner of her eye, she saw Mrs. Adamson watching. She had that same look of concern on her face.

Don't you dare worry about me!

Jules finished playing with the dolls and decided to finish the book she'd started yesterday. Just as the announcement came on to tell shoppers the store was closing, she left the store.

It was hard to come back to herself, to look as if she were just another kid walking home to her family.

Please be there, Dad. Please.

She glanced at the houses on either side of her place before looking at her own.

No, no, no. Oh, Dad.

———

At eight o'clock, Jules went to her bedroom, set up the fort, and lay inside. Craziness crept inside with her. If she fell asleep feeling this way, she might have her awful nightmare again.

She crawled out, sat down by the window, and pulled her knees up to her chin.

The Christmas concert was late this year because the gymnasium had needed repairs. It was all decorated and magnificent now. Each class would come to the stage and perform, just like they'd practiced. Maybe her class was playing their recorders right at that moment. She imagined the joyful notes floating over the audience.

When the concert's over and the lights come on, I bet Mrs. Fournier won't even care I'm missing. Just Patsy. And tomorrow, I'll have to face the mean kids and their nosy questions.

She got a blanket and wrapped it around her body.

Dreams in my head. That's all I ever had.

CHAPTER

11

Another sleepless night.

I can't go to school. If someone asks me why I wasn't at the concert, I'm going to start crying. I'm just going to do what I want today.

She went downstairs, made some toast, and turned on the TV. "Captain Kangaroo" was on. She never got tired of watching that program. Captain Kangaroo looked like what an older father or nice grandfather might look like, might act like.

I'm going to walk to Zellers and play with the toys all afternoon. That's way more fun than being with any of the kids at school.

No, it isn't. I'm going because Mrs. Adamson's there.

It was windy but warmer than the last few days had been. She took her time walking to the plaza. Mrs. Adamson looked surprised to see her. But lots of people were buying toys, and Jules was glad Mrs. Adamson was busy.

Jules played with Maggie – with all the dolls – for a long, long time. By two-thirty, her empty stomach hurt. She went to the book display and picked up a Nancy Drew mystery.

This'll take my mind off food.

She buried herself in the book.

"Hi, Jules."

Patsy's voice.

Jules looked up to see Patsy standing in front of her. She glanced at the store clock.

Four o'clock already!

"You weren't at the concert last night or at school today. How come?"

"I was sick."

"So why're you here?"

"I'm feeling better."

"Oh." Patsy looked at Jules as if to say, "I don't believe you." But Patsy knew better than to ask too many questions.

"Patsy, Patsy, wait up." Rosey walked over with a worried look on her face, pulling Marcus behind her. "Look, it's too hard taking care of Marcus in the store. He's wandering all over the place. Besides, we gotta get home."

"Okay. See you at school tomorrow, Jules?" Patsy asked.

"Sure," Jules said, not looking at her.

Patsy and Rosey took Marcus by the hand and walked down the aisle.

Jules watched.

Patsy has problems. But at least she's not alone. I'm as alone as ever a person could be.

Jules tried to concentrate, to keep her eyes on the words in the book, but she couldn't. Tears dropped onto the page.

Not here. Not in front of people. What a baby I am. What a stupid —

"What's wrong, honey?" Mrs. Adamson was suddenly there, crouched down in front of her.

Few people ever spoke to Jules in a warm soft voice. It caught her off guard and made her cry harder.

"Come to the back, where it's quiet." Mrs. Adamson stood up and put out her hand.

Jules couldn't look her in the face, but she took Mrs. Adamson's hand as she got to her feet. They walked to the back of the store, through a set of swinging doors, and paused in front of one marked STAFF.

"Wait here a minute." Mrs. Adamson went inside.

Minutes later, a few employees came out. Some stared at Jules. Others continued on with their conversations.

Mrs. Adamson held the door open. "C'mon in. I've put the kettle on. Let's have some hot chocolate."

I shouldn't be here. I don't want to talk to anyone.

———

Mrs. Adamson shut the door behind them and got a chair for Jules. She pulled down two mugs from a kitchenette cupboard and filled them with instant hot chocolate. They waited in silence for the kettle to boil.

When the hot chocolate was ready, Mrs. Adamson handed a mug to Jules. "Here. You'll like this."

I don't like anything.

Jules couldn't look at Mrs. Adamson, but she took the mug and held it in her lap. Its warmth felt good.

"Why weren't you at school today?"

None of your business.

Jules kept her mouth shut, her head bowed.

How can I ever tell?

Mrs. Adamson brought a chair close to Jules and sat down. "I know something's wrong, Jules. I . . . just want to help. I . . ." She paused. "Life can be so hard, and if you're young and if you're alone, things seem harder. I sure know all about that."

How can you possibly? Nobody can.

Mrs. Adamson sat quietly beside her for a long time. Jules was glad she didn't try filling up time with empty words.

"Jules, something's not right. It might help to talk about it."

Alone, alone, alone.

"Jules?" Mrs. Adamson asked softly.

If I say nothing, you'll give up.

"Tell me what's wrong."

Won't you ever stop asking?

"Nothing!" Jules said too loudly. "Nothing," she repeated, strangling a sob.

"I've never seen you so sad."

Jules was shocked.

It's a secret, my sadness.

It was frightening, terrifying, to think Mrs. Adamson could see it. Nobody ever noticed anything, except maybe Patsy. No grown-up ever talked to Jules like they wanted to find out what was on her mind or what was bothering her. Most people thought she was a moody kid. She'd heard her father say that enough times to his friend Hank, and Hank sure seemed to agree.

She looked into Mrs. Adamson's face.

Adults only see what they want to see in a kid. Why should I be honest? I know how to fool people. Why let a stranger into the rotten part of my life? Besides, if I say anything, if my words go out into the air, it'll make everything real.

Mrs. Adamson put an arm around her.

How can a stranger be like this to me? To Jules, the stinking weirdo?

If Mrs. Adamson had been mean, Jules could have kept silent, but kindness made Jules's feelings crash together and burst out.

"My dad. He's left me. Doesn't want me."

"What do you mean, 'doesn't want you'?"

"He got mad at me last Friday night and called his friend. They went out, and he hasn't come back."

"Friday night?" Mrs. Adamson looked away, and

Jules knew she was thinking about all the days that had passed since then. "That's a long time, Jules."

As if I don't know.

"Do you know where your dad's friend lives?"

"No . . . yes. But I don't really know how to get there."

"How about where your dad works? Do you know the telephone number?"

"Yes. Dad's got it written down somewhere for me. But . . ."

"You didn't call?"

"No."

"Well, maybe I could."

"No!" Jules shouted, pulling away from her.

"It's okay, hon. I won't, I won't." Mrs. Adamson looked up at the ceiling and took a breath. "All right," she finally said. She held Jules as she stared at the wall in front of them. It was decorated with Christmas cards. "Has your dad ever stayed away so long?"

"Weeknights, sometimes, and weekends, too, when he's dri —" Jules caught herself. "When he's with his friends. But not longer than two nights in a row. This time, I think he doesn't want to come back. He's fed up with me."

Anyone else would say, "No, no, Jules, that can't be true," when they didn't know anything about her life.

"Okay, hon. Okay." Mrs. Adamson was silent again. She looked like she was having trouble knowing what words to use. "I'm sure you can manage on

your own. In fact, I suspect you're pretty amazing."
She looked at Jules with a half-smile. "But you
shouldn't be on your own every day."

*She says I'm amazing. It feels good to hear someone
say that.*

But a heavy, dark feeling was taking hold of her.

Silence is bad, speaking up is bad.

"Nobody should tell my dad and me what to do,"
Jules said in a mean voice.

"Of course not. But . . . sometimes people, families,
need extra help just to stay together, to keep going.
I know that myself. And . . . I know you're strong,
stronger than almost any young girl I've ever met.
But even strong kids shouldn't be alone for so long.
Don't you think?"

Jules didn't know what to say. As young as she was,
she knew that – unlike most kids – she was beyond
needing to be looked after by anybody. Not because
she wanted it that way, but because that's how her
life had been for the past few years. Nothing could
change her back into a kid who needed to be told
when to eat dinner or what clothes to wear.

But she was tired.

"Could you sit here for a few minutes? By yourself?
Will you promise to stay here? I'll be back in a sec.
No one will bother you."

I don't want to promise anything.

Jules's first impulse was to run away the minute
Mrs. Adamson left the room. She started to plan how
she could get out of the store quickly, without being

seen, but she didn't move her body to make it happen.

While Mrs. Adamson was out of the staff room, every so often another employee would pop their head in, say hi, and ask Jules if she wanted anything. Was she hungry? Did she want any more hot chocolate?

"No" was all she could manage to say.

This isn't right. I don't like strangers being kind to me for no reason.

Mrs. Adamson finally came back. She talked about Christmas, and Jules kept her mouth shut.

This is a huge mistake. I'm in for it now. From strangers. From my dad.

After twenty minutes or so, there was a knock on the door.

Mrs. Adamson got up and opened it. "Hi. I'm Sophie Adamson," she said. "C'mon in."

Jules looked at the woman who entered the room.

"Hi, Jules," she said gently. "My name's Eileen, Eileen Ward. And I'm a social worker."

PART TWO ZOMBIELAND

CHAPTER

12

Jules left the store with Eileen, walking through it feeling ashamed, like a criminal.

Eileen told Jules she was going to take her to a safe place, where she'd be looked after, and took Jules home to get some clothes. In the car, she explained more about Catholic Children's Aid.

Jules found it impossible to say more than yes or no to Eileen. Her mouth was dry, and her tongue felt swollen.

It was terrible having a stranger, a social worker, come into their house.

I feel like I'm under arrest.

"I don't need you," Jules cried out suddenly, in a panic, her voice breaking. "Get out! I'm not going anywhere. I have to be here for when my dad comes back! He's coming back. You can't take me anywhere. You can't!"

"It's all right, Jules. It's okay. I'm only here to help you and your dad. And part of my job right now is helping you find him. I'm going to leave my contact information for him, both here and at his work, so he can get in touch with me when he comes back. I know you're very worried about him. But you can't be on your own." Eileen kept looking around the shabby kitchen as she spoke.

I'm always on my own, you idiot. I don't need anybody to look after me – except my dad. Get the hell out of here!

Jules sat down in a kitchen chair and wouldn't move. "No, I'm not going," she said. She held on to the seat of the chair with an iron grip.

Eileen found a beat-up suitcase in her father's closet, but Jules refused to pack any of her clothes. Eileen had to do it.

No. No. No.

Eventually, Eileen got Jules – somehow – to move, to walk out of that house. She used words that were meant to be kind, about finding her dad and helping them both, but mixed in were words about the law and Catholic Children's Aid. The outside world was grabbing her, reaching in and pulling Jules away from her dad, her life. And there was nothing she could do about it.

Eileen drove Jules to downtown Toronto. She explained that they were going to an emergency home, where children like Jules stayed after they were taken by Catholic Children's Aid. Jules had thought she was going to be put in some kind of orphanage, but it turned out to be just an old house on Roncesvalles. Mrs. Currie was the owner. As they walked through the front door, children seemed to be screaming and running everywhere. Jules barely noticed anything else.

Help me, somebody. Help me. I have to get out of here!

Mrs. Currie gave Jules something to eat, but Jules pushed the food away. Eileen sat down with Jules and began asking a lot of questions about Jules's dad and their life together. She even asked about her mom. Jules just shook her head *yes* or *no*.

I'm not going to say anything. Not going to betray my dad more than I've already done.

Jules wasn't going to talk about his angry moods or the endless drinking. And yet these were the things Eileen wanted to hear about – like she was a detective for the bad in people. Eileen also asked Jules about the bruise on her cheek, about whether her dad or anyone else hurt her.

Dad spanks me sometimes. So what? Lots of parents spank their kids. You're turning him into a bad man.

Eileen left around seven-thirty. Mrs. Currie was watching TV in the living room with the other kids. Jules told Mrs. Currie she was tired, and Mrs. Currie took her up the narrow, creaky stairs to the second floor, showed Jules where the bathroom was and where she was supposed to sleep.

Jules stood in the middle of the bedroom, hearing nothing as Mrs. Currie spoke to her. The room was hot, stuffy. The smell of bleach was strong, and when she breathed in, Jules could almost taste it on her tongue. Toys were scattered across the wooden floor. Two blue dressers flanked the large window, which looked out onto the street, and crayon scribbles covered every inch of the gray-white walls. Jules's small suitcase rested on the bottom bunk of the bunk bed against one wall.

As soon as Mrs. Currie left her, Jules changed into her pajamas and opened the bedroom door before lying down on the bunk bed. She listened to the sounds of TV and people moving around downstairs. An hour later, two boys and a young girl came up. The boys went into one room, and the young girl came into Jules's room with Mrs. Currie. Mrs. Currie turned on the light. The little girl, Trudy, who looked to be around seven, fought with Mrs. Currie about having to go to bed, making enough noise to wake the dead. Jules pretended to be asleep.

Morning was chaotic. The boys were arguing at the breakfast table as Mrs. Currie shouted at one of them – Jimmy – to get ready for school. The noise woke Trudy up, and she went downstairs. A few seconds later, she was back in the room with Mrs. Currie, who pulled Trudy's wet sheets off the bed. When Mrs. Currie tried to get Trudy to change out of her wet pajamas, Trudy began to scream.

Jules curled up on the bunk and stared at the wall. She refused to get up.

At ten o'clock, a babysitter came to the house to watch the other kids. Mrs. Currie announced to Jules that — like it or not — she had to get out of bed and go with her to a doctor's office. "They just need to look you over, Jules. The doctor will check your weight and height, that kind of thing."

I've never been to a doctor in my whole life, and I don't need one now!

Mrs. Currie told Jules that she'd be in and out of the office in two minutes. But she lied.

Jules frantically pushed the nurse's and doctor's hands away from her whenever they tried to touch her, grabbing hard, shoving them away with all her might. She almost knocked the nurse to the floor.

"Relax, Jules. We're not going to hurt you," the doctor kept saying. "We just want to make sure that you're okay, head to toe."

No. Don't. You can't. Don't touch me!

"Now calm down, Jules," the doctor said, sounding frustrated. He turned to the nurse. "Just keep her still, would you? C'mon, kiddo. Don't be afraid."

Jules would've made herself disappear off the face of the earth if she'd had the power.

When they got back to Mrs. Currie's house, Jules walked up to the bedroom and slept on and off for most of the day. At dinner with the other kids, she pretended she couldn't hear or speak, so that nobody would talk to her. Afterwards, she quickly retreated to her room.

On Saturday morning, the other kids helped Mrs. Currie wrap presents in the kitchen, on the huge wooden table. When Mrs. Currie told Jules she couldn't stay in the bedroom all day, Jules parked herself on the chesterfield in the living room and watched TV without taking anything in.

Eileen telephoned at noon to tell Jules she'd found a foster home for her. "It's a miracle I found a place so fast, especially one that's near Our Lady of Peace. You won't have to go to a new school."

Jules felt as if her stomach were grinding glass. She'd completely forgotten about school or anything else – except her dad. She wasn't herself anymore. She was just a stupid kid whose life got turned upside down by complete strangers in ways she couldn't have imagined.

I don't need to worry about having nightmares at night. I've got wide-awake ones now.

"Why do I have to go to a foster home?"

"Let's talk about it when we meet up, Jules."

"But my dad –"

"I still don't know where he is, Jules. I haven't heard from him."

December 23. Monday.

"I'm sorry we haven't had another chance to talk," Eileen said when she came to pick Jules up. "It's a crazy time of year."

I don't want to talk.

"Your dad phoned my office this morning."

My dad! He's back! He's back! I can go home!

"Apparently he's been at a friend's — Hank's. He stayed there the night he left. Then he stayed with another friend, someone he met at a party. He hasn't been to work, which is why we couldn't reach him there."

He didn't phone or try to see me. Maybe he doesn't want to be with me — whether he's back at home or not.

Eileen was staring at her.

Stop it! I'm not some freak! All I want is to go back home. Be with my dad. Don't you understand?

"I know how hard all this must be. You might blame yourself for what's happened. But that would be wrong. I know you love your father and he loves you, but you deserve to be a child and to not have to worry about all the things you've had to worry about. You don't deserve to be afraid or hurt or alone. No one does."

I've never hurt this much, and I've got a lot more to worry about now.

"Why can't I just be with him?"

"We're going to work hard to make that happen. I'll be meeting with your father right away to talk over everything and see how we can get you back together. Your dad and I also have to go to family court."

"Court?"

Court equals police equals arrest equals prison. What have I done?

"Please, don't be upset, Jules. Family court's not

what you think. I'll explain more about it as we drive to the foster home. I'm going to take you there now."

Am I supposed to say yes?

"I wish I could have set up a visit with your dad sooner, but it's a hectic time for everybody – the foster parents, the Chapmans, in particular. And your father's not . . . at your place. So he'll be coming over around eleven-thirty Christmas morning. After Mass. Everything's all arranged with the Chapmans, and he'll stay for about two hours. But he can phone you anytime, Jules. He said he's going to call tonight around seven."

"Why can't I just go home?"

It was Eileen's turn to look as if she didn't know what to say. "Your dad . . . he said that he's moving, and –"

Moving? Hell!

"We've had to move before," Jules interrupted. "Lots. We can find a place."

"He's staying at his friend Tracie's for now."

Who's Tracie?

"So this is the best we could work out until he's more settled."

Christmas is over. Over.

"I have a few days off for the holidays, Jules, but next week, I'd like to plan for us to talk again."

Don't bother.

Eileen tried to talk about court again, about what would happen there, but Jules stopped listening.

Eileen changed the subject to school and friends.

School and friends don't matter. I want my dad.

"Here we are."

Eileen parked the car in front of a redbrick, two-storey home on Botfield Avenue, not far from Our Lady of Peace school. It was a large house with big windows surrounded by elaborate white wooden shutters. Evergreens grew on either side of the house, and burlap covered the front yard's small shrubs.

I'm not getting out of the car.

After her experience at Mrs. Currie's, Jules didn't want to be in any foster home. Getting out of the car meant she agreed with being in one, meant she agreed with what was happening to her.

But after five hundred times saying no to Eileen, Jules finally got out of the car.

Eileen was a good person, Jules could tell. But she could make her voice and words commanding, like a teacher's, and Jules knew she had to obey.

She followed Eileen up the five concrete steps that led to the small open porch. Eileen rang the doorbell.

An older woman answered it. "Oh, hi. C'mon in. Is this Jules? How *are* you? I'm Mrs. Chapman. Good to have you."

Mrs. Chapman was a short and stocky woman who spoke in a singsongy, happy voice. She had a bright smile on her face – but it disappeared as soon the introductions were over. Her short white hair was tightly permed, and she wore a striped housedress in pink, green, and gold.

"The girls are out shopping. They'll be back in the afternoon, so that gives us time to get you settled," she said as she bent down and pushed her face close to Jules.

"The girls" better not be elementary school students.

"So this is our home. We're busy with Christmas, of course, but we're happy to have you," Mrs. Chapman said cheerfully as they entered the hallway.

"I'm so glad you could manage it, Eleanor," said Eileen.

"Yes, well . . . in one door and out the other. That's usually how it goes. We're used to it." Mrs. Chapman turned to Jules. "All right, hon. Let's just put your things in your room, and I'll show you around quickly. Okay?"

Okay, okay, okay! Can't I ever say no?

Mrs. Chapman led them around, upstairs and down, talking nonstop. Jules's "room" was on the second floor. The girls' bedroom was beside it. Mr. and Mrs. Chapman's bedroom was on the main floor.

"Eleanor," said Eileen after the tour, "I have to go soon."

"Sure thing. Start putting your things away, Jules, while I talk to Eileen for a minute."

Eileen turned to Jules. "If you have any problem, you can call me at this number." She gave Jules her card. "Or just let Mrs. Chapman know what it is,

and she'll help you with it or get in touch with me."
She gave Jules a hug and said good-bye.

Jules carried her small suitcase up to the bedroom
she'd been assigned. It was bright and sunny.
Spotlessly clean. Smelly clean. Old-fashioned
flowered curtains framed the window, which faced
the house next door. It gave a partial view of the
street. A crib was against the opposite wall. There
was a large empty closet, a small rocking chair in
one corner, and a battered dresser. The bed had a
large wooden headboard, and a worn white
bedspread covered the small mattress. A doll rested
on top of a pillow. Not a play doll. It was made of
cloth, a Raggedy Ann.

Jules heard Eileen say good-bye to Mrs. Chapman.

*I'm back with strangers. Although Eileen's a stranger,
too.*

Mrs. Chapman came upstairs and stood in the
doorway. "All right," she said in a businesslike way,
looking around. "Oh, shoot. Forgot about that crib.
We usually have much younger kids. I'll get Mr.
Chapman to move it to the basement later. Now,
let's see what you've done. Hmm. Why don't we
arrange your clothes a bit better? We'll put some in
the closet, others in the dresser."

I don't want to put anything away.

"Now, have a seat there on the bed," Mrs. Chapman
said once the clothes were unpacked. "I'll run
through a few things. It's as good a time as any, isn't
it? We've got some basic house rules I'd like you to

obey." She took a deep breath. "No helping yourself
to food in the fridge or cupboards, no staying up
late, no making a mess in your room — or anywhere
else in the house, for that matter. Friends can't come
around without permission, and there's no going
anywhere on your own without checking with me.
And no going into anybody else's bedroom or
messing around with my daughters' things."

What can *I do?*

"They're such busy girls. Marilyn's fourteen and
Veronica's sixteen," Mrs. Chapman said with obvious
pride. "And with schoolwork, clubs, friends — well,
they don't need us bothering them, do they? And I
expect you to help out with chores. Just like my
girls. Like any member of the family." Mrs. Chapman
looked at her watch. "Right. Almost lunchtime. Let's
go downstairs and get something to eat."

Mrs. Chapman made Jules a sandwich and some
soup, but Jules found it hard to swallow. While Jules
was eating, Mrs. Chapman went to the basement and
brought up a few books and games.

"Something to read and play to pass the time.
Most of it's old stuff the girls don't want."

When Jules had finishing eating, she reluctantly
picked up the pile of books and games and went
upstairs.

Around three o'clock, she heard a door slam.

"Hey, Mom, we're home!"

"Jules! Jules!" Mrs. Chapman called. "Why don't

you come down? I'd like you to meet Veronica and Marilyn."

Marilyn was taller and thinner than her sister, even though she was younger. They both had big, backcombed hairdos and wore lots of makeup. Their duffle coats were open, so Jules could see the puffy mohair sweaters and pleated skirts they were wearing.

"Hi," they said together.

"This is Jules."

"Neat name," Marilyn said.

"Do you kids want to watch TV together?"

"No, Mom," Veronica said. "We've got to wrap Christmas gifts."

"Okay. Dinner'll be early today. Right after Dad gets home."

"Why don't you watch TV, Jules, while I make dinner?" Mrs. Chapman asked as she watched her daughters head upstairs.

Anything to feel normal.

Sitting in one corner of the big sofa in the living room, though, Jules felt anything but.

This can't be happening.

Mr. Chapman came home at four-thirty. He was short and stocky, too, with a bald head and pleasant face. He wore a simple suit and tie. "Welcome, welcome," he said to her quickly as he popped into the living room and popped out again.

He must be used to having strange kids in the house 'cause he's sure not surprised to see me.

After a few minutes, he came back to the living room wearing an old check shirt and faded black slacks. Without saying anything more to Jules, he started reading the newspaper. Jules kept her eyes on the TV.

Across from her, in the huge front window, stood a large aluminum Christmas tree. Mrs. Chapman had told Jules they put it there so that people on the street could see it lit up at night. It was adorned with only blue lights and golden bells, but the rest of the room was decorated with Christmas knickknacks of every size, shape, and color. A dish on the coffee table held hard Christmas candies.

It's like being inside a Christmas display window in a department store.

At dinner, in between eating mouthfuls of meatloaf, Marilyn and Veronica asked Jules what grade she was in and what kids and teachers she knew at school. Nobody asked about her family or her dad, as if they already knew. Jules didn't want to talk about her cruddy life, but not talking about it made her feel like she didn't have one.

Veronica left the table quickly after dinner to get ready for a Christmas party.

Marilyn sulked in the living room because she wasn't going to one of her own.

Mr. Chapman watched TV.

Mrs. Chapman washed the dishes.

Jules stood in the kitchen like a piece of furniture and dried them.

Six-thirty.

Dad. Can you forgive me?

Six-forty.

Please don't be mad.

She forced herself to watch TV when the dishes were done.

Please call, Dad.

"Jules! It's your father!"

The phone hung on a wall in the kitchen. Jules managed to walk there without breaking apart.

"Dad?" She could barely get the word out.

"Don't cry, honey. It's okay. Everything's going to be all right."

"Dad, oh, Dad –"

"I know, Jules. I know, hon. I'm sorry."

He'd never said sorry to her before. She couldn't breathe.

"C'mon, Jules. It's okay. Everything's going to be all right."

"I want to come home, Dad."

"Sure, sweetheart."

Jules held on to the phone cord as she sank to the floor. Her cries were catching in her throat.

"Enough, hon. This is just a huge mix-up, you know? I mean, you've been on your own before. I knew that." The sadness in his voice was thinning out. "I don't believe what's happened. I just don't. What business does anybody have calling Children's Aid? You didn't steal anything, did you?"

"No, Dad. Never. I'd never do that."

"So why'd somebody call? I don't get it. And why at the plaza?"

I can't tell you.

"One day . . . one day, Dad, I didn't go to school. Maybe —" She didn't know how to finish.

I'm going to throw up.

Her dad didn't seem to know that Mrs. Adamson had been the one to call.

"Geez, you've always been okay on your own. Weren't you, Jules? You're a big girl."

That wasn't the problem.

"Yeah, Dad. I'm sorry. I'm sorry." Words and cries came out together.

"I know you can look after yourself. Hey, you're almost twelve, for God's sake. Jules, you still there? Jules!"

"Yes."

"C'mon, honey. Calm down."

"I'm trying."

I need to know. I need to ask him.

"Where were you, Dad?"

"Didn't they tell you?"

"You were at Hank's, then somebody else's."

"Yeah, you know how it is. Been away lots of weekends."

You didn't want to come home.

"But there was a party, and I met somebody," he went on quickly. "Thought I'd just stay with her a day or two. Her name's Tracie. And before you know

it . . . geez. I get home, you're not there, and social
workers are after me. Christ! Here I am talking to
you at some goddamn stranger's place!" Then lower,
softer, he added, "Are they treating you okay?"

Please take me away from here.

"Answer me, Jules."

"Where are you now, Dad?"

There was a moment of silence. "Tracie's. I guess
the social worker . . . what's her name?"

"Eileen."

"She told you I came here, right?"

"She said you called her from home."

"It's so weird, don't you think? I never heard of
kids getting picked up by Children's Aid at a
department store."

"I didn't mean it to happen."

He let out a long, deep sigh. "Well, what's done
is done. Here they are thinking you're all by yourself.
And as if that isn't bad enough, now the greedy
landlord's squawkin' at me 'cause I can't pay the rent.
I gotta be out of our place on New Year's Eve, if you
can believe it. Good riddance is all I can say. Right,
Jules? I mean, it wasn't the best place to live, eh?"

"No."

"So . . . I'm gonna stay here for a while."

"At Tracie's?"

"Yeah."

"What about me?" she whispered.

"Don't worry, hon. We're gonna sort it all out. I
just need time to catch my breath. And I have to go

to family court. Did Eileen talk to you about that?"

"Yeah, but I don't understand. She said Children's Aid can't take . . . a kid without going to court and telling some judge why they did it. But I . . . we don't have to worry. They won't put you in . . . " Jules took a breath. "You're supposed to go and talk to the judge, and you and the social worker, everybody together, decides what to do. But you're my dad. Why do we have to? Why can't I just come home?"

"Stupid rules. But we gotta play along, or they'll come down on me worse. Everything'll work out. You'll see."

Jules wanted to know exactly how things would work out, exactly what would be happening and when. But she knew from experience that her dad wasn't going to explain. He never talked to her about anything important – and maybe he didn't understand what was going on, either.

"Look, we're going to be together on Christmas Day. That's all that counts."

Jules started crying again.

"Hey, kiddo. Don't do that. We'll have a good time together Christmas morning. Just you wait and see."

I want to believe it.

"Okay, Dad," she whispered.

"So I'll see you at eleven-thirty. The day after tomorrow. Christmas Day! Won't that be great?"

"Yes."

"And you be a good kid. Don't get all moody like

you do. And mind what they tell you. I don't want to hear about any problems."

"Sure, Dad."

"All right, hon. I gotta go. We'll be back together soon. You'll see. Bye."

"Bye, Dad." Jules stood there after he hung up, staring at the phone handset.

Mrs. Chapman came into the kitchen.

She's been listening.

Mrs. Chapman looked at Jules for a moment before speaking. "I'd like you to take a bath and get ready for bed now."

Maybe Mrs. Chapman figured out that foster kids get upset after phone calls from their parents and just want to be alone. If that was true, Jules was grateful.

She cried hard in the bathtub while the water was running and did silent crying while she washed.

He said sorry. Maybe he isn't going to blame me. It was so good to hear his voice. I wish he wasn't staying with someone else. I hope Tracie doesn't like to drink as much as he does.

Jules woke up early feeling unsettled, her stomach in knots. It was Christmas Eve.

After breakfast, Mrs. Chapman asked her to help with some last-minute baking. The girls had gone out. Jules didn't have a clue how to bake anything and goofed everything up. When she dropped the shortbread dough on the floor, Mrs. Chapman ordered her into the living room to watch TV.

The Chapmans had invited some of their friends
over for the evening. Instead of a sit-down dinner,
Mrs. Chapman served all kinds of snack food and
baked goods. Both Veronica and Marilyn had invited
friends over, too.

More strangers.

"Can I go up upstairs?" Jules asked when people
started arriving.

Mrs. Chapman gave her a surprised look. "On
Christmas Eve? Heavens no!"

Jules scrunched herself into the corner of the sofa
nearest the hallway. Every time someone new arrived,
she could hear Mrs. Chapman mumbling something
about her. When she introduced Jules officially in
her jangling voice, she just said, "This is Jules!"

Veronica and Marilyn ignored her completely.
Their friends kept looking at her as if she were going
to fly around the room or sprout fangs.

They'd ask about my stupid life if they had the chance.

Jules got away from everybody as soon as she
could, saying she was sleepy. She sat on the bed,
leaning against the headboard.

*If I put one end of the bedspread over the headboard
and bring the other end to the foot of the bed, maybe I can
make a half-fort.*

When she tried, it worked well, but her mind kept
going back to her dad. No matter how hard she tried,
she couldn't dream her way out of that night.

She got up, knelt by the window, and looked
outside. On the Chapmans' street, many of the houses

were decorated for the holiday. Many of the outside
Christmas lights still twinkled in the darkness.

Tonight everything feels strange, unfamiliar. Without
end.

CHAPTER

13

Opening their gifts, Veronica and Marilyn were as excited as little kids. Their mom and dad and grandparents had given them piles of presents.

Jules got some, too. A book – a Nancy Drew mystery – and some chocolate.

"But I have nothing to give you."

"That's okay," everyone said. "Don't worry about it."

"Time to get ready or we'll be late for nine o'clock Mass," Mrs. Chapman announced. "Jules's father is coming around eleven-thirty."

The girls were in their own world, comparing gifts, trying on clothes, and complaining about having to fast before Mass.

Jules despised the fact that she had to go to Our Lady of Peace church with them.

Everybody in the parish is going to find out I'm with

the Chapmans and start asking questions.

Luckily, they arrived late and had to sit at the back. Jules kept as far away as possible from the Chapmans in the pew. After Mass, Mrs. Chapman chatted and gossiped for a long time on the church steps – while Jules hid behind Mr. Chapman.

"Why don't you come help me with breakfast, Jules?" Mrs. Chapman asked when they finally got back.

After the baking disaster, Jules could tell that Mrs. Chapman didn't want her in the kitchen, but she didn't know what to do with her, either.

I'm a wind-up toy. Turn the key. Point me here. Point me there.

When breakfast was over, Mr. and Mrs. Chapman stayed in the kitchen drinking coffee. The girls went up to their room.

Eleven-thirty came.

Eleven-forty.

Eleven-forty-five.

He's late! Christmas morning and he's late. After everything that's happened!

The doorbell rang at ten to twelve.

Her father looked tired. His large eyes were bloodshot, and his face was pale. But he'd shaved and put on his church clothes. He carried a brown paper shopping bag filled with presents.

Jules ran to him and held him, burying her head in his jacket. "Dad! Dad! Dad!" Her voice kept rising each time she said the word.

"Hey, hey, settle down, Jules!" Mr. Chapman said in an enough-of-that voice. "It's Christmas morning, for heaven's sake. No need for hysterics."

"That's right, Jules. It's okay, honey," her dad said. "It's okay." He looked up at Mr. Chapman with an embarrassed smile, extending his hand. "Hi. I'm Joe Doherty."

"Bill Chapman."

They exchanged Christmas greetings, but Jules was deaf to them. Her arms were still wrapped around her father.

I'm not letting go.

Mr. Chapman invited him into the living room. Mrs. Chapman came in from the kitchen, introduced herself, and asked if Jules's father wanted coffee or tea.

"Coffee'd be great."

"Okay, I'll just get it ready. And then we'll let you two have your visit."

Mr. Chapman disappeared. Jules and her dad were alone in the living room.

"Please don't be upset. I'm sorry for what happened. I know it's awful, but everything's going to be all right."

Jules couldn't speak.

"We gotta get over this. It's really a big mistake. You know that, honey."

She nodded into his chest.

"Well, look at this living room, would ya?" His voice sounded strange. "Look at all the Christmas decorations. You must be in heaven."

Keep holding me, Dad. Don't let go.

"Are you okay? How are they treating you?" he whispered as he looked into her eyes.

How can I begin to answer?

"It's okay, Dad. But I want to come home. Please let me. I can't stand being here."

"I know, sweetie, I know. I want you to come home, too. But there's things that have to be worked out first."

"You mean about being here?"

"Yeah. It's stupid, but once you're in a foster home, there's things you have to do to get back together. Didn't Eileen explain?"

"She tried, but I don't understand."

"That's okay. This is going to blow over. It's nothing. Things are going to be good – better – when we're back together."

"I can't be here, Dad. Please, I want to come home," she sobbed.

"As soon as I can straighten things out." He was starting to sound frustrated. "I don't get it. I mean, an eleven-year-old's not a little kid. And you had a place to live."

"I don't understand, either, Dad. I don't know what they're doing to me."

Words and cries mixed together. Jules always tried to crush her emotions around her father, but she couldn't today.

"Hey, that's enough."

It took only one look from him. Jules knew she'd have to stop crying.

"We're not gonna get through this, honey, if we go crazy. God, I feel like a little kid myself, having to report to those damn social workers, looking for a job and a new place. But today's Christmas, and it's time to have our own little celebration. So let's stop worrying, eh?"

"Don't you work at Thompson's anymore?"

"That foreman," he said in an irritable whisper. "Such a big shot, big mouth. Always breathing down my neck. Couldn't cut me some slack when I took time off. I'll get another job. Easy. I always do."

He was a good mechanic. But that wasn't the problem. He was finding it harder and harder to keep a job once he got one.

"It wasn't a good place to work. And I'm clearing out of our house," he said, looking almost happy. "Getting rid of the extras we dragged around with us — 'cause there's no room at Tracie's. Can't wait for you to meet her. She's been great."

He'd had girlfriends on and off. That wasn't unusual. Most of them liked to drink, though. And if they hung around the house too much, they got on his nerves. Those times could be scarier than the drinking parties.

"Things'll be easier now that Tracie's around."

Jules didn't know what to say. Moving meant she might have to go to another school. She'd lose her friends. "Do we have to move again?"

"I told you about the landlord already. Besides, I can save money by being at Tracie's, and that's a big help. Especially now."

"Couldn't I be there, too?"

He looked away and grabbed the bag of presents. "It's just one room in a house. Too small."

Mrs. Chapman brought in the coffee and left quickly.

"Enough talking, kiddo. C'mon, let's sit down and open these gifts." He placed the shopping bag on the floor beside the couch.

"But I couldn't get you anything. I didn't have any money." Her dad had usually given her a few dollars to buy presents.

He reached over and touched her cheek. "Don't worry about me. Let's have our Christmas." He handed the bag of gifts to Jules. "Merry Christmas, sweetheart."

"Merry Christmas, Dad." Jules put the bag down and gave him a long hug.

"Hey, you've waited long enough. Open those presents!"

She pulled the wrap off the first one. A board game. Clue.

"Great, Dad. Thanks."

The next present was big.

My doll!

It was a hollow chocolate Santa.

"Don't eat it all at once."

"I won't."

She opened the last gift, a jigsaw puzzle of Santa Claus flying with his reindeer.

"That'll keep you busy for a while."

"It sure will."

How many times did I tell you about the doll? How many? It's the same price as all these gifts. Why didn't you buy it for me?

"Man, I wish we didn't have to meet here. Not much to do, huh?" he said, looking around the room. He finished his coffee. "Sure is Christmassy, though."

He's getting bored.

"Do you want to play the game? It looks like fun."

He looked at his watch. "Sure, Jules. They told me the visit could go for only two hours, though, and I might have to leave early. I gotta be back by two o'clock. Tracie and I are going over to Hank's for Christmas dinner."

Jules didn't like Hank. He was always unfriendly and acted as if she was a pain to be around, even though she was only a kid. And whenever her dad came back from a party at Hank's, if he came home at all that night, he was usually too drunk to do anything.

It was weird playing a board game with her dad. He tried to be interested in it, but Jules could tell he wasn't.

Doesn't matter. He's come back to me, and we'll be together again.

When the game was over, he looked at his watch. "Gotta get going, hon. It's one-thirty. I bet you're gonna have a great Christmas dinner. Better than anything your dad could whip up."

"Oh, Dad. I want to be with you."

I'm more alone than I've ever been. Don't you see that?

He gave her a hug. "And I wanna be with you, too, Jules, so don't worry. Things are gonna be fine. You'll see." He stood up and headed to the kitchen to say good-bye to Mrs. Chapman.

At the front door, Jules put both arms around him again – tight – and wouldn't let go. A blast of icy air hit them as he struggled to open it.

"Hey, no more scenes. C'mon. They can hear you. They won't like it." He pulled her arms away, bent down, and gave her a last hug.

As soon as he left, Marilyn and Veronica came bouncing down the stairs, and the house came back to life. Later in the afternoon, friends and relatives of the Chapmans started arriving. In total, seventeen people sat down to Christmas dinner. Jules Doherty was one of them.

She'd never had such a Christmas Day, had never seen a dinner like the one before her – glistening roasted turkey. Mountains of mashed potatoes. Sweet potatoes with maple syrup. Baby peas with mint. It was almost like the kind of dinner people on TV had, where nice families with nice houses had nice Christmases. More fuss, mess, and noise went into preparing the food than anything Jules had ever experienced.

Jules couldn't bring herself to be part of the talk and laughter at the table and felt none of the joy she saw in people's faces. Nobody really talked to her. She meant nothing to them, after all.

At the first opportunity, she escaped.

In her own world, the one that was gone, she could have made her fort and disappeared into dreams. Even though it had been difficult to do when there was so much trouble around her, the power to change everything in her mind, to imagine, had always been there.

But for the past few days and all through that long Christmas Day, she'd had to be something she wasn't – a foster kid. Acting like that person wrung her out.

Images of strange people, strange surroundings, how her dad looked and acted, were upsetting, disturbing. They threatened to smother what she was; steal parts away.

She'd have to fight to hold on because her dreams were all she had.

In my mind, I can fly around the world or go to the moon. Fight dragons or monsters. Sail on the ocean in fabulous sailing ships, soar into the night sky without wings. I can go to planets no one has heard of or ever imagined, places with orange skies and yellow mountains that are inhabited by creatures no one has ever seen before. Wonderful places where I have wonderful adventures.

In my mind, I can be an Olympic athlete, a millionaire. A knight, wizard, or sorcerer. A fighter, hero, or inventor. A princess or witch, a butterfly or bumblebee. I can speak any language, look like any person, live in any time. I can conjure up fairies, trolls, giants, or any magical creature I want.

In my mind, I'm smart and brave, able to save the world. I can lead armies, create fabulous music, imagine warm and cozy homes in places so beautiful it hurts just to look at them.

In my mind, there are people who see me, Jules the person, and love me anyhow.

CHAPTER

14

On the twenty-eighth of December, the Saturday of Christmas week, Jules had another visit with her dad.

Hank gave him a ride over so he could bring bags of Jules's clothes, most of her toys and books, her recorder, and her skates.

"I'm moving," he said to Mrs. Chapman by way of explanation. He looked tired and thinner than usual.

Jules got angry when she saw an old doll peeking out of one of the bags, so angry that she grabbed the bag and – without saying anything to her father – ran upstairs.

He shrugged his shoulders as if to say, "Kids!"

Mrs. Chapman helped him carry up the rest of Jules's stuff.

"Boy, isn't this nice?" he said, looking around the room.

Jules couldn't look at him.

I want to scream!

"I wouldn't have brought everything all at once like this, but I've got no room where I'm staying."

They went downstairs again, and Mrs. Chapman prepared coffee as Jules and her dad sat in the living room.

"Seems like a nice lady."

I'm not going to talk to you. You never understand me.

"Knock it off, Jules. I'm not going to put up with one of your lousy moods. I'm going through a rough time, and the sooner you get that, the better."

Jules held her breath.

"So, Christmas dinner was good?"

She nodded and stared at the floor.

"Dammit!" he said, raising his voice. "I'm leaving this minute if you don't talk to me!"

He wins. He always does.

He stayed for only an hour, promising as he left that their next visit would be better.

It was harder than ever for Jules to know what to do with herself when Christmas and Boxing Day were over. Marilyn and Veronica had a lot of friends, and they either went out or invited them to the house and hung out in their room.

Jules helped with the chores, watched TV, or stayed in the room her things were in. Mrs. Chapman complained to Jules that she was underfoot too much.

"It's not good to stay in here all day," she said one morning. "You should be going out. Don't you have *any* friends?"

I can't face the kids I know. I'd be a stranger to them.

"I'll have to tell Eileen that all you do is mope around."

What should I do? Where should I go?

She worked up the courage to phone Patsy.

"Where were you, Jules? I've been phoning your place like crazy."

"Dad and I weren't home a lot."

"Boy, I thought you were really sick or something."

"Nah."

Jules didn't want to talk over the phone and asked Patsy if she could go over to her house. Patsy had to babysit, but as long as they included her brother in whatever they did, it'd be okay.

Jules got permission to go, gave Patsy's telephone number and address to Mrs. Chapman, and took off. She felt freer than she'd felt in a long time, though she had a big knot in her stomach at the thought of facing Patsy.

"So where were you?"

It took everything in her to tell Patsy the truth.

Patsy tried to keep the shock and worry out of her face. She was never very good at hiding her feelings, though. "That's awful, Jules."

Awful doesn't come close.

"But they found your dad. Why can't they let you go back?"

"Parents get into trouble for going off and leaving their kids."

Jules didn't want to talk about the drinking and some of the more terrible things that had happened. It was too much to tell anybody.

And no one in the world would have found out if I hadn't been weak and stupid.

"Eileen, the social worker, told me she went to court to ask a judge to allow them to take me . . . away from my dad. And now he has to go there and do what they say to get me back." She couldn't tell Patsy they'd been kicked out of their home. "Besides, he's not working right now, and he has to get a job."

Patsy didn't say anything for a while. They were sitting on the bed in her room, the one she shared with her sister. She looked at Jules, then down at the bedspread and began picking at some of the fraying threads like she was trying to yank them out.

It's one thing to be scared. It's another when your best friend is scared for you.

"Gee. Over Christmas, Jules. And you gotta stay with people you don't even know."

Strange how Patsy's the only one who speaks the truth.

CHAPTER

15

*F*oster.

Jules knew the word but wondered why it was used to describe what she was, what Mr. and Mrs. Chapman were. She looked it up in an old dictionary she found in the Chapman basement. "Foster: to bring up or nurse; to encourage, to promote; to cherish."

Cherish.

Jules spent a long time in the bathroom the first morning of school after the holidays, searching her face, trying to figure out if what had happened to her — what she was — showed. It was January 6, the day of the Epiphany.

My face is pale, colorless, as always. My eyes look as if they're bulging out of my head, like my soul is trying to escape my body. If I keep my eyes down, maybe they won't notice.

"Jules, you're old enough to make your own lunch," Mrs. Chapman told her when she got downstairs. "I have enough to do. I've left out what I want you to have."

Bread and bologna. Ha!

When she got to class, Mrs. Fournier gave her a knowing look.

Shut up. If you say anything, I'll kill you.

None of the kids in her class acted differently toward her. Yet. It was good being back at school, though. She didn't expect to feel that. She could pretend she was normal for at least part of the day.

Jules asked Patsy if she wanted to come over to the Chapmans' after school. Having Patsy inside that house with her might be good. Her old regular life could soften the new, and she might not feel so out of place.

"Nice house," Patsy said as they walked around to the back door.

"I guess."

It felt pretty bare inside after all the Christmas decorations were put away. The furniture wasn't old or run-down, but there wasn't much of it. Mrs. Chapman was always complaining about how she needed a new this or that – washing machine, car, clothes for the girls. Mr. Chapman said they'd be able to afford a whole lot more if their kids didn't have to go to a private Catholic school.

Mrs. Chapman said he was welcome to pull them out, but it would have to be over her dead body.

"They're going to be raised properly, to be ladies, if it takes every last penny we've got!"

Mr. Chapman dressed like a businessman, and Jules thought every businessman had money, but maybe the insurance company he worked for wasn't successful.

The Chapman family really was like the families her dad talked about, the ones who had fancy-looking houses on the outside but ate Kraft Dinner every night on the inside.

Jules and Patsy found Mrs. Chapman in the living room, watching TV. A soap opera.

"This is Patsy, my friend."

"Oh. Hi there," Mrs. Chapman said without looking away from the screen.

"Can she stay over and play?"

Mrs. Chapman looked as if she'd just been zapped by a monster mosquito. "Well, Jules, you know what I told you. You should check with me first."

That's what I'm doing.

"I like to know ahead of time."

"It's okay," Patsy said quickly.

Mrs. Chapman looked at Patsy. "Some other day."

"Can I show her the room?"

"Of course."

There wasn't much to see. Patsy stayed only a few minutes.

As soon as the front door closed, Mrs. Chapman called out from the living room, "Now get yourself changed and start your homework – if you have any."

Jules was starving. "Could I have a sandwich or maybe an orange?"

"We're going to have dinner soon. I don't want you to spoil your appetite."

Jules went up to the room and made her fort.

What can I imagine? It's white all around me. I'm in a snow castle, standing on a battlement, a knight looking below to where the enemy troops gather. . . .

Thump!

"What's that noise? What's going on up there?" Mrs. Chapman yelled from downstairs.

Jules picked herself up off the floor, went into the hallway, and leaned over the banister so that Mrs. Chapman could see her. "I was sleeping. Fell out of bed."

Had my nightmare again.

"For heaven's sake, Jules! What a lot of noise you made. And look at you. Haven't even changed out of your uniform. Please get it off." Mrs. Chapman turned her attention back to the TV.

When the girls got home, Jules heard them turn on "American Bandstand." She forced herself to go downstairs. Marilyn had brought a friend home.

I wonder if she has permission.

They all said hi when Jules came into the living room and sat down.

"This is Jules," Marilyn said. "One of our foster kids."

"How many do you have?"

"Just her. But we always have one or two around."

"Oh."

Jules felt her face get hot.

"She's at Our Lady of Peace. Grade 7."

"How was it? Today at school?" Jules threw the question out into the room, hoping either Marilyn or Veronica would pick it up.

Veronica didn't. She kept her head stuck in a *Seventeen* magazine.

"The usual," Marilyn replied and began talking to her friend about volleyball practice.

When "American Bandstand" was over, the three of them left Jules and went upstairs.

"Jules had a nightmare today. Screamed blue murder and fell out of bed," Mrs. Chapman said, laughing, as they ate dinner. "Gave me quite a shock."

"Oh," Mr. Chapman said. He looked at Jules as if she were one of the blocks of wood in his basement workshop.

"I'd have nightmares too if my father —"

"Veronica!"

"Well . . . ?"

"Jules just had a bad dream, didn't you?" Mrs. Chapman said.

Jules hung her head over her plate.

That night, she couldn't calm herself down. The rocking chair was near the window. She could have turned it sideways so that she'd be able to sit and look out, but Jules hated rocking chairs. When you sat in one, you had to move back and forth, unless you used your legs and feet to keep the chair still. But that wasn't relaxing.

She preferred to rock her body to her own rhythm, wrapping her arms around her ribcage and holding on.

Taking a blanket from the bed, she sat on the floor in front of the window. The window was too high for her to see outside very well, unless she knelt by the sill, but she could still see parts of the sky.

The moon might be there. Stars or clouds. But outside it's dark. That's all that matters. I'll send my thoughts out of me, set them against the night sky, and try to leave them there.

It was possible to do. It had always been possible to do.

CHAPTER

16

January 18. Saturday. Jules waited for her dad.

She didn't have a watch. She didn't need one to know when he was supposed to show up. She'd been downstairs in the kitchen, sitting by herself, but she'd had to come up because her thoughts were crashing against the walls.

The phone rang.

"Jules, Jules, it's your dad," Mrs. Chapman called up from the kitchen. "He wants to talk to you."

She came downstairs slowly and took the phone.

"Hi, honey."

"Hi."

"Uh, I'm sorry, Jules. Tracie and I were supposed to get a lift with Hank, but he never showed up. Too late to get there now. But I promise I'll be there next week."

"Okay."

"So, what're you going to do today?"

Nothing. Nothing. Nothing.

"Probably play at Patsy's or Teresa's."

"Good. That's good. Okay. Have a nice time, and we'll see you next week. We'll have fun."

"Yeah."

I'm not going to let you hang up yet.

"Dad . . . you went to court, Eileen said."

"Yeah."

"She said I'm a ward, in the care of Children's Aid for three months."

He sighed into the phone. "Not even that, you know. It's temporary, just for now. Until I get myself sorted out. So don't worry about it one bit. We can talk about it when we meet up."

"I miss you, Dad."

"Miss you, too, Jules. Gotta go. Bye."

Jules couldn't say good-bye, couldn't look at Mrs. Chapman as she hung up the phone.

My chest and stomach hurt. If I have to stay here the whole afternoon, I'll go crazy. The plaza. I'll go to the plaza.

Mrs. Chapman gave her permission to go, plus fifty cents spending money.

She headed out into the cold.

A part of Jules wanted to be angry with Mrs. Adamson – for all time. But another part knew that Mrs. Adamson hadn't meant to make her life miserable.

As Jules pushed the door open to Zellers, her heart beat faster. She felt as if all the employees were staring at her. She kept her head down. She could get to where she wanted to go without looking up.

Candy department first. No candy canes, Christmas candies, chocolate Santas – except for some stuff on a table shoved to the side. Half price. Discarded.

Then the toy department. Mrs. Adamson was at the cash register. Jules wandered toward the dolls and stuffed animals. Mrs. Adamson spotted her and rushed over. She looked as if she wanted to grab Jules. Jules moved sideways, so that wouldn't happen.

"It's so good to see you!" Mrs. Adamson said in a loud shaky voice. "I was so worried! How are you?"

Jules did not look up.

"I tried calling Eileen. But with the holidays . . ."

Shut up about it.

Jules started to walk away.

"Stay, please. Um . . . your doll's been moved. We changed the display. It's over there."

"Oh."

"Did you . . . ? You wanted it for Christmas. Did your dad . . . did anyone?"

"No." Jules's lips trembled.

"Are you going to be in the store for a while?"

"I guess."

"I'm going on a break at three-fifteen. Would you like to have a drink at the Canadiana?"

"Uh . . ."

Say yes? Say no?

"I have to be back by four-thirty," Jules said.

"There's enough time. It'll be easier to talk over there. What do you say?"

"All right."

Jules fooled around the toy department and read books, then she and Mrs. Adamson walked to the restaurant. Mrs. Adamson ordered coffee for herself, a pop for Jules.

"I'm so glad you came in today. I was so worried! I couldn't reach Eileen at first. Then I called after Christmas and asked what had happened. But there's only so much she could tell me. It was awful not knowing, particularly . . . particularly because I felt responsible. And I . . . I knew what a hard time you were having. I only wanted to help, Jules. I hope you understand that."

Despite everything, Jules couldn't bring herself to hate Mrs. Adamson.

She really cares about me for some stupid reason. Not like Eileen. Or Mrs. Chapman.

"You're here so often. I thought we'd become friends, and I just wanted to make sure you were okay."

"Okay" is a lousy word that hides a lot. I'm not okay.

"Did you . . . did your dad . . . ?"

"They found him. He came back."

"So you're togeth —"

Jules cut her off fast. "No. I'm in a foster home."

"And your dad?"

"My dad . . ." Jules felt tears rising up. She waited until she could talk. "My dad's staying at a friend's house. We're not going to live in the same place we did. We'll probably move away from here."

So nobody can poke their noses into our business anymore. I need to protect us. My dad's a good person, no matter what anybody says or thinks.

"The social worker told me I have to stay at the foster home, but just until . . . he's ready. Settled."

Mrs. Adamson reached over and touched Jules's hand. "I'm sorry, Jules."

Why? Because Jules and Joe Doherty are screwed up?

"How is it? At the foster home?"

What kind of question is that? I don't even have the words to describe it to myself.

"It's okay."

That stupid word again.

"It can't be easy for you."

If I start to feel sorry for myself or show how sad I am — right here, right now — I'm doomed.

"No."

"And Christmas?"

Tears fought their way back up again. "My dad came over in the morning. It was fine."

She'd never seen Mrs. Adamson act so nervous, look so upset. Maybe she understood how hard it was for Jules to talk about all the bad.

Mrs. Adamson began to ask her about other things, like school and Patsy, and that gave Jules a chance to relax. She told Mrs. Adamson bits and pieces about the past few weeks, only what she wanted to tell.

"My break's almost over. Do you want to come back with me to the toy department?"

"No. I'm gonna go ho–. I'm going to go back."

"You're welcome to stay and read. And look at the toys. You know that."

"I know."

Mrs. Adamson looked as if she wanted to say something more but didn't know how to begin. She glanced shyly at Jules. "Um . . . I've asked Eileen about this, and maybe – if you like – you could visit us, my family and me, some Saturday. I don't work every weekend."

"I visit with my dad on Saturdays."

"Oh."

Today is Saturday.

"Well, maybe on a Sunday then, after church? If it's okay with your dad, of course. I've already mentioned to Eileen that you and I have become friends. So I told her about me and my family and gave her references – that sort of thing. I'd love to have you visit us so we can get to know each other better."

No! I hate everybody and everything. And why would anyone want to be with me, Jules the nothing?

But Mrs. Adamson isn't like other people.

"I guess."

"Great!" Mrs. Adamson gave her a bright smile. "I'll get in touch with Eileen, and we can arrange something."

"Sure."

When Jules left the restaurant, part of her felt good, but another part was aching.

CHAPTER

17

January 25.

"Tracie can't come today. She's gotta work."

"That's okay. We can do something together."

But sitting inside, talking, playing board games — it wasn't them, wasn't how Jules and her father were with each other. They decided to go for a walk.

"Dad, why don't you get a pair of skates? Some skate shops sell them secondhand. We could go to Wedgewood next time. Or the rink on Montgomery."

"You think I wanna wear somebody else's castoffs?"

When Jules was eight or nine, her dad used to get together with his work buddies and play hockey on Saturday afternoons. She remembered standing against the boards of the outdoor rinks they went to, watching him.

Most adults looked like strong skaters no matter what — because they were big. But Jules could tell that her dad stood out from the rest of the men he played with. She'd never seen anyone skate as fast as he did or play hockey so well. He'd been on the hockey team at St. Mike's in Toronto, with a scholarship when he was a teenager, but his mom pulled him out of school to work.

But, oh, today . . . he doesn't look good. And he smells of alcohol. He's only thirty-five, but he looks like an old man.

Jules didn't want him to be around the Chapmans and hated herself for feeling that way.

He was quieter than usual this afternoon.

"So who's this Mrs. Adamson you want to visit? Is she the one who reported me?"

That's what's bugging him.

Jules was silent.

I wouldn't tell him the truth in a million years.

"I don't like it one bit. I was . . . I had too much on my mind when you and the social worker phoned me this week, but now that I think about it, I don't want you hanging around that goddamn store *or* the people who work there. Ever. When I get back to Tracie's, I'm going to call and get the visit cancelled."

No!

"It's Saturday today. You might not be able to reach anybody at Children's Aid. And the visit's tomorrow."

He thought about that for a minute.

He won't want to make a fuss, get in trouble — especially

with people who're interfering in his life too much already.
   He wants to make me feel bad, though.
   "Well, it's creepy, if you ask me. The visit
tomorrow with this department store lady will be
the first and last. You got it?"

CHAPTER

18

The Chapmans were in a hurry. Mr. Chapman honked the car horn.

Mrs. Adamson came outside to greet them at the curb.

"Well, here she is," Mrs. Chapman said from the passenger seat in the car. "Open the door, Jules. I've written down the address and phone number for my sister's place, and here's the number of the agency in case there's a problem."

Mrs. Adamson said hello to everyone and took the piece of paper from Mrs. Chapman. Jules got out.

"And we'll pick her up at four o'clock?"

Mrs. Adamson nodded.

"Great."

The Adamsons lived in a yellow brick bungalow on a small corner lot near Patsy's place. Larger, two-storey homes mixed in with the bungalows all along the street. Jules's dad had once told her that the whole neighborhood got built up after the war, when regular people started being able to buy houses. Most of the rickety old farmhouses, like the one Jules lived in, had been torn down.

From the outside, the Adamson home looked bigger than it was because of the small garage attached to it. The front yard was tiny, and there was no grass in the backyard, just exposed dirt. Mrs. Adamson had told Jules once that the vegetable garden out back was Mr. Adamson's pride and joy. The neighbors called it an eyesore.

"Hang your things on a peg, like we do."

They'd entered through the side door. Stairs led up to the kitchen and down to the basement.

Jules followed Mrs. Adamson up. A huge, old table lined one wall, with mismatched chairs tucked underneath. The lino floor was a checkerboard pattern of black and white, in contrast to the pale yellow walls. Mrs. Adamson went over to the counter next to the sink. There were kitchen cabinets below the counter space as well as open shelves above that displayed dishes, canisters, ornaments, and plants. The room felt cluttered and cramped, bright and warm.

Feels like a home.

"Are you hungry? Did you have lunch? I hope not."

"Uh . . . no." Jules's nerves had made her stomach hurt, so she hadn't eaten.

"Good. We'll have some lunch after I introduce you to Katie. The twins are out skating, but they'll be back soon. That'll give us some quiet time to ourselves. I thought it'd be good with just the three of us. Frank, Mr. Adamson, worked a night shift, so he's still sleeping." She turned to look down the hall. "Katie! Katie!" she called softly.

A little girl about five or six years old came into the kitchen. She had straight dark hair like her mother's, although it was longer, parted off to one side, and held in place with a blue barrette in the shape of a butterfly. She had a wide face with white, white skin and chubby, apple-red cheeks.

"Jules is here, honey. Say hi."

"Hi," Katie said shyly. Her dark blue coveralls fit loosely over a red top that was splotched with snowflakes. She held a small toy dump truck in one of her stubby fists.

"Would it be all right if you and Katie play for a bit while I finish making lunch?"

"Sure."

"Remember to be quiet, though, Katie. Dad's still sleeping."

"Okay." Katie grabbed Jules's hand and led her down a short hallway toward the living room. "I'm playing smash-up."

As she walked behind Katie, Jules tried to get a look at the family pictures plastered on the hallway walls. There wasn't much furniture in the living room – a TV, a worn sofa with no cushions, and a lumpy-looking upholstered chair that didn't match the sofa. An assortment of cars and trucks of all shapes and sizes was strewn about the coffee table in the center of the room.

The sofa cushions were missing because Katie had stacked them on the far side of the coffee table – one on top of the other, like steps. On each step were small cars and trucks that must have tumbled from the coffee table. A toy gas station rested on the floor against the wall with a toy dump truck below the front window. Pieces of a homemade toy racetrack led from the gas station to the tiered mountain of cushions.

Katie grabbed two cars from one of the cushions. They were the kind that wound up if you pressed down on them and pushed forward. Katie wound them up on the coffee table and then watched, grinning from ear to ear, as the cars flew across the table and down the cushion mountain. They crashed on the last cushion.

Katie wound them up again and put them on the track, where they smashed into each other. Then she grabbed the dump truck and carefully used the pulley to load them up and cart them off to the gas station.

Jules picked up a car, revved it on the coffee table, and let go. It flew across the table and into the air, landing on the track.

Katie looked impressed. "It's my turn, my turn." She quickly wound up another car, but it flew off in the wrong direction. "Aw. No good." She looked at Jules shyly. "Can I go again?"

"Sure."

This time, Katie's car had a spectacular crash.

"Wow," Jules said. "That was great!"

Katie giggled and looked very pleased with herself.

Jules got down on the floor and tried to see how far she could make a car go. Katie squatted down beside Jules, copying her, laughing like crazy when their cars collided.

"Lunch is ready!"

Mrs. Adamson had prepared tuna sandwiches and carrot sticks. A large plate in the center of the kitchen table held oranges cut into wedges.

Zombies move their mouths, swallow, drink, but taste nothing. I have to be careful or I'll choke.

Mrs. Adamson looked as nervous as Jules felt. And she was an adult. Katie wasn't nervous at all and babbled nonstop.

"Do you want to see my dolls after lunch?"

"Sure."

"Remember what I told you, Katie. Only after we clear up," Mrs. Adamson said. "I'll get Jules to help with the dishes first."

"Aw, Mom!"

"And you can clean up the mess in the living room."

"Aw, Mom!"

"Aw, nothing. Get going."

Katie reluctantly left the table. Jules helped Mrs. Adamson bring the dishes to the sink.

Now what do I say?

"It's great to have you here, Jules."

Warmth crept in, spreading through her.

"It's easier to talk here than in the store."

Harder for me.

"There's more time to get to know each other, too. I've wanted my family to meet you for a long time."

Can't believe that.

"The two girls I saw in the car are the Chapman kids?"

"Yeah. Marilyn and Veronica. They go to St. Joe's."

"What are they like?"

Strangers.

"I don't know. They're busy all the time. With studying, friends, clubs."

"What kind?"

"Debating society and drama for Veronica. She's in the school play, *The Mikado*. Marilyn plays volleyball and field hockey. I don't see them much."

"I'm glad you'll finally get to meet Jeff and John. Then you'll know who they are when you see them at Our Lady of Peace. Katie'll start there in September."

Hell.

"I hope you can get to be friends. And maybe all of us could go to Wedgewood sometime to skate? That's where the twins are now. Or we could play baseball at the park when the weather's better? You told me once how much you loved baseball." Mrs. Adamson paused. "Lately, though, we never know what day Frank is going to be off. The owners of the furniture factory call him in only once in a while these days, and he needs all the work he can get." Mrs. Adamson went red and looked down at the dishes in the sink. "Sorry. I sometimes forget how young you are."

I know all about dads not working.

Jules dried the dishes as Mrs. Adamson washed. When they were done, they went into the living room.

"Well, Katie, do you think it's time?"

"Yes, Mommy. Yes, yes, yes!"

"Okay, you bring it out."

Katie ran down the hallway and into one of the rooms. She came back, barely able to carry a big box covered in Christmas wrap. "For you!" Katie handed the box to Jules.

Jules gave Mrs. Adamson a puzzled look.

"For you, Jules. A New Year's gift."

Jules sat down on the sofa and stared at the package.

Katie knelt beside her. "Open it, open it! Why aren't you openin' it?"

Jules pulled off the wrapping paper. She knew what it was with the first tear.

My doll. My beautiful doll.

"Why's she crying, Mom? Doesn't she like it?"

"It's okay, Katie. Just let her be."

"Jules, Jules!" Katie said anxiously, gently shaking her arm. "Don't be sad."

Jules couldn't help but smile at her. Then she looked at Mrs. Adamson. She was struggling to stop the tears. Her heart was melting.

"Open the box, open it! Let's see the doll!" Katie said as if trying to cheer Jules up.

With Katie's help, Jules slowly lifted the doll from the box. Gently touching the hair, she examined every inch of the lace and velvet dress.

"It's a beautiful doll, isn't it?" Katie declared. "I love it!"

Jules nodded.

"I got beautiful dolls, too. Lots. You wanna see?"

"Maybe Jules just wants to play with her own doll for now, honey."

"No, she doesn't, Mommy. That's no fun."

"It's okay. I'd like to see them."

Jules carefully placed her doll back it its box and held it tight as Katie led her to her room.

Mrs. Adamson followed and stood in the doorway, watching. Stuffed animals and dolls of all shapes and sizes lay on Katie's small bed and dresser.

"This is Ginger, that's Fluffy. . . ." Katie said, listing off the names.

"Show her Lucy, Katie," Mrs. Adamson said softly.

Katie gently picked up an old porcelain doll from the top of the dresser. The doll wore an old-fashioned linen dress, decorated with blue flowers, and a matching bonnet.

"This is Mom's, but I have to protect it."

"Can I hold Lucy?" Jules looked at Katie to ask the question, but she was really asking Mrs. Adamson.

"Just for a sec. She's *really* old," Katie answered.

Mrs. Adamson smiled and nodded yes.

Jules kept her own doll on her lap and took Lucy. She had never seen a doll like this one before. Or if she had, only in a special display at Eaton's or Simpson's. The doll's face looked like the face of a real little girl, and her hair — done up in tight black ringlets — felt real, too.

Oh, how wonderful!

Jules heard a door open and shut, then loud voices and feet stomping. Within seconds, two boys squished in beside Mrs. Adamson at the door to Katie's room.

"Hi!" they both said.

"Jules, this is John and Jeff," Mrs. Adamson said.

Katie had told Jules the twins were nine, but they looked tall for their age. John was taller than Jeff.

"Hi," she said back.

"Okay, boys. I made your lunch. Go to the kitchen. I'll be there in a sec."

"Can Jules still play with me, Mom? Can she?"

Mrs. Adamson looked at Jules. "Katie's found a new best friend, I think. Okay, Katie, but Jules can stop anytime she wants, and she can play with the boys or just play by herself with her doll."

"Yes, yes, yes!" Katie sang.

"Hey, where's our guest?" a man's voice called from the hallway.

"We're in here, Frank!"

Mr. Adamson came to the door, gave Mrs. Adamson a hug, and peered inside Katie's room. "Well, well."

"Jules, this is my husband, Frank."

"Hi."

Mr. Adamson was slightly taller than his wife. He had red curly hair that looked as if it grew straight up into the air. It made his large head seem even larger. His face was freckled all over.

"Pleased to meet you," he said, smiling broadly as he came into the room and shook her hand.

Jules blushed. No grown-up had ever done that before.

Mr. Adamson was wearing an old dressing gown over pajamas. On his feet were thick wool socks with black heels and stripes running down the white toes – like animal claws. Jules couldn't take her eyes off them. She couldn't believe a grown man would actually wear socks like that. It made her smile.

"So what have you two been up to?" Mr. Adamson asked Katie.

"Playing, Daddy. And Jules has a new doll and she cried when she got it, but she likes it, though, and now we're gonna play with mine."

Mr. Adamson turned to look at his wife, who was still in the doorway. "All right, but you can't have her all to yourself. Maybe she'll want to play with the boys now."

"But me, too."

"Of course, sweetheart." He turned to Jules. "I'd love to stay with you both, but I'm starving. I've got to see if the monsters have saved some food for me." He bent down, gave Katie a hug, and left the room.

Katie went back to telling Jules all about her stuffed animals and dolls.

About fifteen minutes later, John came back to Katie's room. "I got the board game Aggravation for Christmas. Want to play with me and Jeff?"

Jules looked at Katie. "Do you mind – for a while?"

"O-kaaay."

Jules carried her doll back to the living room and set it gently on the sofa. Turning to Mrs. Adamson, she said, "I'm just going to keep it in the box, if that's okay."

"Sure, Jules. Why don't I get you a shopping bag for it? It'll be easier to carry that way."

"Thanks."

Katie demanded to play Aggravation with Jules and the twins, but John and Jeff refused. The Adamson kids started arguing and yelling at each other so much that Jules thought something bad was going to happen. But Mrs. Adamson was able to interest Katie in playing a card game with her. John, Jeff, and Jules went back to the game as if nothing was wrong.

Just after four o'clock, there was a knock at the door.

Mrs. Chapman.

"Would you like to come again, Jules?" asked Mrs. Adamson. "We'd love to have you."

"Come again! Come again!" Katie shouted, jumping up and down.

What can I say? Dad doesn't want me to be here.
And good things never happen to me.

"Ah – sure. I guess."

"Okay. We'll arrange something," Mrs. Adamson said.

Jules squished into the backseat of the Chapman car with Veronica and Marilyn. They wouldn't stop talking about the wonderful time they'd had with their goofy cousins. Nobody bothered to ask what she was carrying.

I don't care. Maggie's perfect, precious. And she belongs to me.

CHAPTER

19

How do you sleep in a bed that isn't yours? How do you accept that the walls, ceiling, and furniture of your room look different? That the view from the window is not the same? That the houses, people, and places you used to see each day are gone — even if they were messed up and crappy? How do you talk to people you don't know, people you have to share almost every living second with?

How do you accept it when the people you love are ripped away?

When Jules was around the Chapmans, she couldn't relax, couldn't even breathe properly. When she was alone in the room they gave her, she curled up on the bed, held her doll close, and tried to calm down. Or she'd lie flat on her back and stare at the ceiling, letting the air out of her body — slowly, slowly.

She couldn't bear to be without Maggie, especially at night.

She's the one thing I can care for in this uncaring place.

Jules didn't take Maggie anywhere else in the house. In the mornings, she hid her in a secret spot in the closet. No one was going to see or touch her.

Each weekday, the girls ate their breakfast with Mrs. Chapman, then left for school. It was a long walk away, so they were gone by the time Jules came down to the kitchen. Mrs. Chapman usually hummed along to the music on the radio while she cleared up. Jules ate in silence.

Mrs. Chapman reminded her of a big bumblebee. She buzzed around the kitchen, bobbing her head to the rhythm of whatever song was on the air. Jules imagined two big antennae on her head, bouncing up and down as she moved – with an eyeball on the end of each to help her see 360 degrees, so that she could catch Jules touching or taking anything that wasn't hers.

Nothing is mine.

Mrs. Chapman's body was round like a bumblebee's, too – with a stinger on the end of it.

She'd say, "We're going to have to buy our own cow if Jules keeps drinking so much milk," or, "Jules is like a cat – hates water and never wants to have a bath." She'd talk that way at dinner and laugh as if she'd just made a joke. The girls would look at each other and smirk. They knew it wasn't funny.

"Get your breakfast and make your lunch, or you'll be late for school. Talk to me when the soap opera's over. Put your uniform in the laundry. Don't fight with the girls over the TV. Where are you going? When are you coming back? Stay away from the fridge. Go out and play. Do the dishes. Clean up the bathroom. Time for bed." That's all Mrs. Chapman ever had to say to Jules.

Mrs. Chapman loved shopping, sewing, watching soaps, and fussing over the girls, her precious girls. She never asked Jules about herself, school, friends, or her dad.

Just as well. She looks at him like he's got a contagious disease.

Jules couldn't say or do anything that felt normal in that house — even though it had been five weeks since she'd come to stay with the Chapmans. And even though she tried to be friends with the girls, some kind of invisible barrier stood between them.

Veronica never answered back right away when Jules spoke to her. It was as if there were a delayed-response button on her vocal cords. She'd stare at Jules first, which made Jules feel like she'd just said something weird or stupid — that if Jules took a few moments to think about it, she'd know exactly why it was weird or stupid. Then she'd say, "What?" — and Jules would have to start all over again.

Veronica studied night and day. After finishing Grade 13, she wanted to go to university. Her world was school, friends, and boys. In that order.

Maybe she thinks I'm childish. Or bad.

Marilyn was interested only in sports and boys.
She was one of those pretty, popular girls who know
who to talk to and who to ignore. Mr. and Mrs.
Chapman gave in to her on everything, even over
Veronica. Mrs. Chapman often said that Veronica got
the brains in the family, but Marilyn got the looks
and personality. They looked at Marilyn with smiles
full of pride, as if they couldn't believe they'd created
a person so unlike themselves.

Marilyn complained about Jules endlessly. "Jules
ate the last cookie! Jules doesn't clean up the
bathroom properly. I want to watch TV with my
friends, and Jules won't leave us alone! Get out of
my chair! Get your hands off that!"

However they acted, Jules could see that Marilyn
and Veronica were happy and moved easily through
their days.

She couldn't help it, but after school sometimes,
she'd sneak into their room and pretend everything
in it was hers.

Mrs. Chapman made a point of telling Jules that
Veronica and Marilyn's bedroom suite was "real
mahogany." A large velvet quilt in white and pink
covered the bed, topped with various throw
cushions. The clothes closet took up almost an
entire wall – packed with clothes, shoes, hats, purses,
magazines, and records. The lovely oak desk that
stood near the wide window on the far side of the
room didn't look like anything that came from a

store. Mr. Chapman must have made it in his workshop.

Veronica and Marilyn had taped pictures of pop singers and movie stars from fan magazines onto the walls. Cliff Richard, the Beach Boys, Frankie Avalon, Bobby Rydell, Audrey Hepburn, Paul Newman, and Elizabeth Taylor were their current favorites. There were also framed paintings, likely done by Veronica and Marilyn when they were much younger.

They have everything they want. So they must have played with dolls when they were little.

Jules didn't find any in their room.

Maybe they're packed away somewhere.

When Marilyn and Jules were at home alone one day, Jules worked up the courage to ask. She knocked on her bedroom door, opened it, and stood at the entrance. Marilyn and Veronica didn't let her come in without permission.

"Yeah?"

"Uh, I got this doll as a present."

Jules didn't want her to see Maggie, but Marilyn needed to know how big the doll was. "I thought some of my old doll clothes would fit, but they don't. Do you have any?"

Marilyn looked Jules up and down. "I'd be more worried about my own clothes, if I were you."

Jules felt as if she'd been punched in the gut.

"How old are you anyway? Eleven? Twelve?"

I know what you want to say. Girls my age aren't supposed to play with dolls. So what? Who made up the rules?

"Eleven."

"When's your birthday?"

"March. March 8."

Marilyn turned back to her textbook. "We got rid of our dolls and doll clothes a long time ago. Gave them to our cousins."

"Oh."

Marilyn must have talked about Jules's lousy clothes behind her back because a few days later, Mrs. Chapman made Jules try on some of Veronica and Marilyn's old clothing that had been stored in the basement. Jules couldn't bear the touch of it against her skin.

"That'll do you fine," Mrs. Chapman said over and over as she forced Jules to try everything on. "And I'd show a little appreciation if I were you, young lady, instead of looking so miserable. Why should I go to all this trouble? You won't get any money from Children's Aid for good clothes like these. I can tell you that."

When she was alone, Jules wrecked one of the dresses. She wished she could do that with each and every piece of clothing – burn the whole pile.

CHAPTER

20

February 8.

In the afternoon, Jules's dad called to cancel their visit. Tracie was going to take him up to Thunder Bay to see her parents.

You cancel after last week's rotten visit? All right, then. I can make plans myself. Just watch me!

Jules called Patsy and asked if she wanted to go to the Cloverdale Mall. In all the time she'd lived in the neighborhood, she'd never gone there alone – it took too long to walk. It was better than the Six Points Plaza because there were lots more stores, and they weren't as expensive as the ones in the Kingsway. The Kingsway was a fancy area for rich people. Her dad liked going there, even when they lived in Mimico, but he never had enough money to buy anything. The only store in the Kingsway for people like them was Woolworth's, and it simply wasn't worth all the effort to get there.

Mrs. Chapman didn't care where Jules went, as long as it didn't cost much. She just wanted her out of the house on the weekends. Patsy got permission, too. She knew how they could get there by bus because she'd gone with her sister, Rosey.

They went into the Hudson's Bay Company first, straight to the toy department – a gazillion times bigger than the one in Zellers. Lots of dolls and doll clothes lined the shelves, and Jules pretended she could buy whatever she wanted. Barbie dolls were becoming really popular. Jules and Patsy liked Barbie well enough, but Jules didn't want a doll that was like a teenager, that didn't need to be cared for or loved like a child.

When the salesclerks started to bug them, they went downstairs to the candy counter. They bought a big bag of Spanish peanuts with the money Mrs. O'Connor had given Patsy, and they ate every last one.

"Argh! I'm so thirsty, I'm gonna die!"

"Me, too."

"If we walk home instead of taking the bus back, we could go to the restaurant near the shoe store, sit down like adults, and get a pop," Jules suggested.

"Terrif. Beat ya there!"

Jules got to the restaurant first.

"Let's pretend we're fabulously rich heiresses and can order what we want," Patsy said when she caught up to Jules at the restaurant door. "You'll be the stunning and brilliant Daphne, and I'm the gorgeous and talented Amelia."

"Gorgeous and talented, you are."

"What shall we do tonight, dahling? Go to the opera? A nightclub?" Patsy drawled as they sipped their drinks in the restaurant booth.

"Well, dahling, I'm sure I don't know."

"We're so very popular. Everyone wants our company."

"But everyone is so dull."

"Especially the boys." Patsy sighed.

"Yes. They're boring and unimaginative."

"Duller than dirt!"

"And here *we* are – beautiful, smart, and brave!"

"Oh, and fabulously wealthy, too – don't forget."

"Dripping with dough."

"That's why we should set off again. Especially. Considering." Patsy gave Jules a knowing wink.

"Considering, especially." Jules winked back.

"Zanzibar. Or South America."

"But that'll tip off our evil stepfather," Jules whispered.

"Yes, well . . . let him be tipped," Patsy replied, then burst out laughing.

Their waitress walked by and scowled, making them laugh even harder. Patsy was giggling so hard, she couldn't catch her breath. Everyone in the restaurant started to gawk.

"Compose yourself, my dear," Jules said, trying to look sophisticated.

"Yes, of course."

"The fact of the matter is, we can't vanish when we're the toast of the town, now can we?"

"We cannot." With her nose stuck up in the air, Patsy raised her glass and — with a dramatic flourish — clinked it against Jules's.

"I think you'll find the champagne delightful," Jules said. And Patsy got the giggles again.

"All right, enough. We must be serious." Patsy said, looking anything but.

"Yes, of course."

"There are more important matters to discuss. The plot to abduct us, for one thing."

"The very nerve."

"Well, Daddy-O wants all our money."

"And us out of the way."

"Out of the picture."

"Out."

"Plain out."

"We have to find his accomplices, or we're done for," Jules said, looking suspiciously at the waitress.

"Done in."

"Roger Dodger that, Kemo Sabe."

They dawdled over their drinks. When they finally left the restaurant, huge snowflakes were drifting down from the afternoon sky. They had a snowball fight on the way home, and it was almost dark when Jules got to the Chapmans'.

Her mind and body were singing.

CHAPTER

21

Jules's dad phoned on Thursday to say that her royal highness would be at the visit that Saturday, the fifteenth.

"I'm one hundred percent sure we'll make it." Her dad sounded happy.

Why is Tracie so important, anyway? What about me?

Tracie was almost as tall as Jules's dad, who was six feet. She was thin — bone thin. Her hair was in a pageboy and so blonde it looked almost white. Her long bangs covered half her face. Jules barely caught a glimpse of her eyes.

"So this is Jules? Good to meet you, kiddo. I've heard a lot about you."

"How about giving Tracie a hug?" her dad suggested.

Jules didn't want to, but did anyway. Tracie

smelled of cigarettes, alcohol, and perfume. Jules felt only bone.

Her dad turned to Mrs. Chapman. "We'll be at the fish-and-chip shop at Bloor and Ashbourne."

"All right," Mrs. Chapman said. "Have a good time."

It felt good to walk down the street with her father, even if Tracie *was* on the other side of him.

"How's school? Your dad says you're pretty smart." Tracie didn't look at Jules when she spoke. *Maybe she's not used to kids.*

"It's okay. Kinda boring sometimes."

"So, what do you like to do when you're not at school?"

"Skate. Play with my friend Patsy, my dolls."

"Dolls? Aren't you a little old for that? You'll be thinking of boys and makeup pretty soon." She laughed. "Those were the days. Had the time of my life when I was your age. You're a nice-looking kid. The boys'll be getting interested, whether you like it or not."

All right already!

"Dad, Mrs. Adamson gave me the doll I told you about, the one at Zellers. For a Christmas . . . a New Year's gift. It's wonderful. Do you want to see it when we get back?"

"Why'd she do that?" he asked angrily. "You hardly know her."

"That's not really true. You know, I go . . . I

used to go to the plaza all the time. She's always there. I told you."

"Yeah, and I told you not to have anything to do with anybody at that goddamn store!"

"I know . . . I don't, but . . ."

"It's stupid. Doesn't she have kids of her own?"

"Yes," Jules whispered.

"Well, I'm not going to tell you again. I don't want you going there. And I don't want any more strangers poking into our lives. You hear me?"

He'd raised his voice enough that even Tracie looked worried. Jules wondered if she knew who they were talking about. Or if they talked about Jules at all.

"Hope this place isn't far from here, Joe," Tracie said.

She's trying to get him off the anger track.

"You know I hate trudging through snow."

"Don't worry, we'll get there soon enough."

The fish-and-chip shop served mostly takeout customers. Jules and her father had never eaten there, but when he hadn't felt like getting groceries or if the power had been cut off, he'd pick up an order – or send Jules.

"What're you gonna have, Jules?" her dad asked.

They were sitting at the table closest to the back wall. Tracie and her dad sat side by side facing her.

"Just one piece of fish. And maybe we can share the fries?"

"Where's that killer appetite?"

Jules knew she was supposed to smile, but couldn't. She looked down at the plastic tablecloth.

"You doing okay at the Chapmans'?"

She nodded.

I hate being there, Dad. Please let me be with you.

"And school's okay?"

"Yeah. Math's kinda hard right now."

"How come?"

"Too many kids in the class. Mrs. Fournier's always too busy."

"Well, you'll get it eventually. Just keep working hard."

We never talk like this.

"Are you far away, Dad – where you are? I mean, you and Tracie?"

"You could ask Tracie that."

No, I can't.

"C'mon, Joe. Don't be hard on her."

"We're in the old neighborhood – in Mimico – right on Royal York."

"Oh."

How do I get there? How far away from me are you? Tell me, Dad. Please.

"It's small, but good."

"It's small all right," Tracie said. And they both laughed. "More like a closet, but cozy."

"Glad to be out of that cruddy farmhouse we were in. Not very good, was it?"

"No. But where are we gonna go?"

He shot her an angry look.

He's not going to tell me. I can't breathe.

Jules almost knocked her chair over as she got up. "Uh, Dad, I have to go to the washroom."

"Go ask one of the guys behind the counter where it is."

"No, I . . . they're busy. It's too hot in here anyhow. I'll go over to the variety store."

She raced out of the shop and turned to the right, past Ashbourne Variety, and all the way to the opposite end of the small strip mall. She pressed her body against the outer wall of the building.

No. No. No.

The world was smashing, crashing down, the ground bursting open. She was going to collapse, fall, break into pieces. Tears fell.

I have to hold myself in.

Jules wrapped her arms tightly around her body.

A mother and child were waiting for the light to turn green at the intersection of Ashbourne and Bloor. They stared at her.

My face is red. My eyes are red. He can't see me like this.

She forced herself to move and entered the variety store. The older woman behind the counter owned it with her husband. They spoke to each other in another language – Italian or Greek, maybe. The woman was friendly enough, but she always acted as if she thought customers were about to steal something. Jules never would have done that, and it made her mad to be suspected.

"Um, I'm sorry, but do you have a washroom I could use?"

Jules tried to keep her face down as she asked the question. She could tell the woman wanted to say no right away, but – after looking at Jules for a moment – she changed her mind.

"Okay. You come here."

Jules followed her to the back of the store. The woman pointed to a door. "Quick. You be quick, huh?"

Jules nodded.

She couldn't look at her face in the bathroom mirror. Head bent, she turned on the cold water tap and splashed water against her skin, got toilet paper, wiped her face dry, took a deep breath, and forced her gaze up.

I'm still here.

She pinched her cheeks so the redness around her eyes wouldn't stand out. Cupped water in her hands. Drank.

Better.

Her father watched her walk through the fish-and-chip shop.

Yes, I was crying.

When the food came, Tracie ate little, picking at it. She looked as if she was trying hard to think up things to say.

Jules's appetite was gone.

Tracie lit a cigarette and took a long drag. She kept looking at the customers who were coming and going as she drank coffee and smoked. Her bright red lipstick left a mark on the yellow end of the cigarette. It was the wrong color for her skin.

"You feeling better now, Trace?" her dad asked.

"Much better. The coffee's kicking in."

They talked and laughed about what they'd done the previous night.

Jules watched them.

Some bony, skinny people aren't born that way. They like drinking more than eating. Like my dad. Tracie's face is flushed, like my dad's, and puffy, too.

Her father checked his watch when they were finished eating. "Almost one-thirty. We gotta get you home, kiddo."

Walking back, Jules stayed close to him. "Do you talk to Eileen often?"

"Talk to Eileen? When I can get her on the phone! But she's pretty clueless. I bet she doesn't even have a kid, and here she is telling me what to do."

"I'm sorry."

All this started because of me.

"Yeah, well, they can only go so far. People gotta live their lives. Don't need anyone telling me how."

It took fifteen minutes to get back to the Chapmans'. As they walked, Jules reached for his arm and held it. "I hope you can get a job soon."

"Always the little worrywart." He looked at her and smiled. Then the guilty look he'd had throughout the visit came back into his face. "Our troubles are gonna blow over. And, in the meantime, you're living in a nice place, and you're clean and warm, and they're looking after you properly. That's all that counts."

When they reached the front door, her dad bent down and gave Jules a kiss. Tracie gave her a hug.

"Do you wanna come in?"

He looked at his watch. "Next time, hon. We'd have to have coffee or something. I don't want to miss the bus."

"Okay."

They said good-bye, then her dad and Tracie turned and walked down the street without looking back.

CHAPTER

22

The following Monday after school, Jules went to the plaza. She got as far as the door to Zellers.

On Tuesday, as far as the cosmetic counter.

Wednesday was a cloudy, gray, miserable day.

Thursdays aren't for endings. Fridays are.

Mrs. Adamson was at the cash register with a customer when Jules reached the toy department. Instead of waiting for Mrs. Adamson to come over while she played with the dolls and toys, Jules forced herself to walk up to the counter and wait. She prayed that nobody else would need help once Mrs. Adamson was finished.

"Hey, Jules! It's great to see you." A smile, like sunshine. "Have you had a chance to check with Eileen and your dad about another visit? We're going tobogganing on Sunday, and it'd be great if you could come."

Tobogganing.

"Uh . . . my dad, he said that maybe . . ."

"Yes?"

". . . I shouldn't visit."

"Visit who? Us?"

"Yeah. He thinks what I did . . . the trouble . . . he thinks I shouldn't be hanging around the store. Things have to get settled first."

Jules felt the sadness creep up out of her and into Mrs. Adamson.

"Sure, Jules. Of course." Mrs. Adamson looked as if she didn't know what to do with the papers in her hand. She turned away and stared down at the cash register.

I can't cry. I'm not going to cry.

"I didn't say anything to him, about who —"

"It doesn't matter, hon." Mrs. Adamson looked into Jules's eyes. "Please don't worry about that."

Of all the people in the world — and "all" means only one or two — I don't want to say something to you that's bad. I love my dad and need to make sure we'll be together again.

"Uh, my dad . . . he's good. Things'll be okay soon."

A woman came to the counter, dragging a kid in the middle of a tantrum.

"I understand. Really. Maybe more than you

think. I didn't have it easy growing up . . . I don't mean to say . . . I know you love him, Jules. And I hope everything works out. You're a very special girl."

Special nothing.

"It'll be soon, I think. We're going to move and —" Jules stopped. She could feel her face getting red. She didn't want the customer to hear their conversation. Didn't want to leave. "I don't know when, exactly. And maybe, probably, out of this neighborhood. Back to where we were before. In Mimico."

"If you don't mind . . ." the woman with the child said impatiently to Jules. "If you're not buying anything . . ."

"Please, we'll just be a moment," Mrs. Adamson said, trying to put on the face she used for customers.

Jules looked at the child, who was rolling around on the floor, screaming.

If only I could act like that.

Mrs. Adamson reached for Jules's hand.

Jules pulled away and ran.

"Wait, Jules, wait!"

"She's not even buying anything!" the woman said to Mrs. Adamson. "Oh, for heaven's sake, Joanie," she pleaded with her daughter. "Would you please stop!"

"I'm sorry," said Mrs. Adamson. "I can't . . ." She left the counter and caught up to Jules near the exit.

This will be the last time.

"I'm so sorry, Jules. But I want you to know this . . . I want you to hear me. If you ever need me – ever – I will always –"

"I know."

CHAPTER
23

Jules's birthday landed on a Sunday, but since nothing was open, she and her dad decided to celebrate the day before, March 7. She was so excited about the visit that she decided to forgive him for missing the last two Saturdays.

"Why don't we go to the Kingsway and have lunch at Woolworth's?" he'd suggested over the phone. When they lived in Mimico, they'd sometimes go there as a special treat.

He arrived at the Chapmans' late. Jules had been waiting for him in the kitchen, watching the hands on the clock not move. She barreled out the door past him as he stood in the hallway, so that he wouldn't have to talk to Mrs. Chapman. He reeked of alcohol, even though he acted sober. In one hand, he held a small rectangular parcel.

Hurray! Doll clothes for Maggie.

Whenever the subject of her birthday had come up, Jules tried to tell him she wanted doll clothes. The ratty old clothes from her other dolls didn't fit. Maggie was special, and Jules wanted to keep her that way.

"My present!"

"Hold on, birthday girl. Open it when we get to Woolworth's."

It was a bright sunny day. Slush and snow still covered everything, but winter was melting away.

Jules didn't want to ask her dad if he'd gotten a job, or talk about Tracie, Eileen, or the Chapmans. *Nothing bad!*

Once they were on the bus, he asked about school – like he'd done when they'd gone out to lunch before. But after a while, they ran out of things to say. Jules watched the people on the bus or looked through the grimy bus windows at the passing streets.

I'm with my dad, me and me alone. He has a present for me, and we're going to eat yummy food!

Just before they got to the lunch counter at Woolworth's, her dad pulled her aside. "I've only got five bucks," he said with an embarrassed laugh.

"That's okay. We don't have to eat anything. Just have pop."

"No, no, it's your birthday. We'll get a drink each plus one other thing, okay?" He grabbed her chin. "C'mon. No worried faces."

They sat down at the snack bar.

"So, Jules Doherty's turning twelve. And growing

like crazy. You won't want to be around your old
man pretty soon."

"Don't say that."

"Well, happy birthday, hon."

He passed her the gift, and she ripped off the
wrapping paper.

A makeup bag.

"What's wrong?"

Jules fought to keep the expression on her face
right.

"C'mon, you don't know what's inside. Open it!
There's real lipstick in there, a small bottle of
perfume, nail polish. The works!"

*Anyone who knows me — anyone! — knows that makeup
is the last thing I want.*

"Dammit, Jules. The least you could do is say
thank you."

"Oh, thank you, Dad. I —"

"What?" His voice was loud.

"I like it. It's just . . ."

The waitress approached.

Her dad ordered for them. "And gimme that
coffee quick, eh?" He pulled out his cigarettes. A
long mirror ran along the entire back wall of the
snack bar. He looked at himself for a moment, then
looked away. "For Christ's sake, Jules. Somebody
goes to all the trouble of getting you a special present,
and you act like it's crap."

*That "somebody" wasn't you. It was Tracie, and
Tracie doesn't know the first thing about me!*

If they'd been at home alone, her father would've thrown the cosmetic bag in the garbage. As it was, he tried to yank it away from her, but Jules wouldn't let him.

"No, Dad. I like it. Really. It's just that —"

"It's just that it's a stupid present."

"No. I'm not used to . . . I never thought —"

"No, you never thought. You never do."

The day's going bad.

Jules forced herself to pull out the lipstick and take off the cap. Red. The kind Tracie wore. "Gee, it's a pretty color."

The waitress brought over the coffee and pop.

Jules opened the tiny perfume bottle and sniffed. "Wow, it smells great — like roses! Here, have a sniff."

He took a few sips of his coffee. Then he slowly turned his face toward her outstretched hand and smelled the perfume. "Better put the stuff in the bag. Don't get it all over the counter."

"I can hardly wait to try it all out."

"That's bull, and you know it!"

He kept smoking, drinking coffee, and facing away from her on purpose. She wished their food would come to distract him.

Jules oohed and aahed over the big plate of fries the waitress brought. She gave him some to eat, gobbed with ketchup — just the way he liked them.

When they were finished, they walked slowly along Bloor, looking in shop windows. Jules told him about the game she played with Patsy, the one where they pretended to buy whatever they wanted. He started to play along, and his mood got better.

When they were near the bus stop at Montgomery Road, he said, "I may as well say good-bye, Jules. The bus'll take you straight to Botfield."

You can't go yet.

"Why don't we walk some more? It's fun."

"Not much else to see beyond this point. And if you miss the bus, it could be forty minutes before the next one comes along. You know what it's like on Saturdays."

It's my birthday.

He gave her a hug, but she held herself frozen like a statue. When he called out "Happy birthday, Jules!" in a happy voice as she got on the bus, she didn't turn around.

She was glad there wasn't a free window seat.

When she got to the Chapmans', she ran upstairs to the room and threw the makeup bag against the wall, hoping the bottle of cheap perfume inside would break.

The Chapmans "celebrated" Jules's birthday at lunch the following day. Patsy wasn't allowed to come.

"We'd like her to be here," Mrs. Chapman said. "But I'm going to my sister's right after lunch, and the girls will be busy. We don't want you two to be alone in the house."

Mr. Chapman was going to be in his workshop,

but that didn't seem to matter. He floated around the house half the time like a stranger, too.

Mrs. and Mr. Chapman gave Jules a pair of "good" matching gloves and scarf for Mass. She received another Nancy Drew mystery from the girls and a blue beret from Eileen, which Eileen had brought over earlier in the week.

Mrs. Chapman had bought her a birthday cake, and everyone sang "Happy Birthday." Marilyn and Veronica stuffed down their piece of cake in seconds. Veronica was in a hurry to get to a friend's to study, and Marilyn was going skating at Montgomery.

Jules asked her if she could come along.

Marilyn looked at her mom as she answered. "No, I'm meeting Barb. Sorry."

Mrs. Chapman immediately started humming a song and clearing off the table. Jules felt like a dummy and went upstairs. The good feeling she'd had – with their singing to her, getting cake and presents – died.

CHAPTER

24

*H*ow am I supposed to get through each day when my life feels like it's stalled, stopped, frozen in time? I feel like I'm moving through muck at zero miles an hour.

In early April, Jules's dad called to say he'd found a new job.

"It's at a car dealership on the Queensway. Got it made now. Only thing is, I might have to work some Saturday mornings."

"That's okay. We can have a visit later in the day."

"Yeah, but by the time I get washed, on the bus, and over there, it'll be too late."

"We can switch to Sunday then."

"Sure."

But one thing or another – work or Tracie or Hank – kept getting in the way. He started to telephone more than visit.

As if I've gone away.

Jules asked her dad for the phone number at Tracie's place, and she started to call often.

"I need to know, Dad, ahead of time – about the visits. So, if you can't come, I'm not stuck by my –"

"Hold on there," he interrupted. "It's not my fault. Half the time, I don't know myself."

"Sure, Dad. It's just –"

"Nobody's stopping you from doing whatever you damn well want."

"But sometimes it's too late to make a plan with someone else."

"Listen. I told you already. It's hard for me to know – either it's overtime or something else pops up unexpectedly. I'm the one dropping everything and coming all the way."

"But can't you just call me Friday night?"

"That's the one night I have to enjoy a break. I work hard, you know."

In the middle of April, they walked to Jules's empty schoolyard for one Saturday visit. Another day later in the month, they stared at each other in the Chapman living room.

I hate living room visits!

CHAPTER

25

"Get your uniform off," Mrs. Chapman called to Jules every day after school as she came in the back door.

Jules would make her way quietly through the kitchen, sneaking food as Mrs. Chapman watched TV. If only one or two apples or oranges were left in the fruit bowl, Jules would leave them alone. She didn't want the usual lecture about spoiling her dinner or – the recent favorite – not being considerate of others. It was harder to sneak bread or cookies, but over time, she got better at it.

She'd lug herself upstairs, throw her schoolbag on the floor, change out of her uniform, and take Maggie from her hiding place. If she was falling-down tired, she'd slip under the bedcovers and sleep – a good thing if she wanted to escape, but bad if she wanted a proper night's sleep later on. Night in that room was awful.

The girls got home later than Jules did. They were always busy with after-school clubs. Dinner was at five-thirty, when Mr. Chapman returned home from work.

Jules had to clear the table or help with the dishes. Most of her other chores were done on the weekend. Mrs. Chapman said she was training her girls – and Jules – to be good homemakers, although the training didn't include teaching Jules how to cook. Mrs. Chapman didn't want Jules anywhere near the kitchen.

Mr. Chapman would turn on the TV after dinner. He got first choice, the girls second. Mr. Chapman liked watching Red Skelton, "The Garry Moore Show," and westerns. Marilyn loved "The Patty Duke Show" or anything about teenagers.

Jules went up to the room if she was bored or lonely.

At night, it helped if she played with Maggie or read a book. Playing her recorder reminded Jules of Christmas and missing the school concert, so she didn't practice anymore. Reading was better. It helped push the past and present away and stopped Jules from having her own thoughts. She'd make her fort, bring the lamp under it, get Maggie, and read until one or two o'clock in the morning.

Even so, she had her nightmare often. It was basically the same dream over and over – Jules as a shadow, trapped in a world she couldn't escape.

CHAPTER
26

Jules had only one visit with her father in May. And one in June. The days passed, each one feeling longer than the one before it.

But summer finally came. Veronica and Marilyn got summer jobs.

Hallelujah!

Veronica worked as a day camp counselor, and Marilyn was hired as a waitress at her friend Barb's family restaurant. Jules did her chores – and theirs, too. When she complained, Mr. and Mrs. Chapman said the girls were working and she wasn't. It was the least she could do, they told her, especially after all they were doing for her.

Veronica and Marilyn banned her from the basement when they had summer parties and from the backyard when they sunbathed and played badminton with their snooty friends. Jules was sick of feeling like a blob from outer space in that house, stuck in another time warp, while Marilyn's and Veronica's lives happened all around her.

Mrs. Chapman spent her time flitting around the house most mornings, or she went out shopping, came back, made lunch, and watched soaps in the afternoon. Jules thought she'd be able to move, stretch out, and relax with the girls working, but Mrs. Chapman wanted her out of sight.

To make matters worse, Patsy went away in early July to her aunt's cottage for three weeks.

An eternity!

When the emptiness of each day drove Jules crazy, or when she felt like she was the only person left on the planet, she went to the plaza and wandered around. Sometimes she'd stand in front of Zellers, her face against the glass, looking in. Other times, she'd sneak inside. Jules never went right to the toy department and never stood where Mrs. Adamson could see her. Instead, she went to the lipstick-testing counter in cosmetics or to the candy department. She could watch Mrs. Adamson and Frances working or talking to each other from both places.

How come I miss people more than they miss me? How come I carry those feelings right smack in my face — and other people don't seem to?

Jules didn't like it that Mrs. Adamson looked

normal. She wanted to be able to look at her and see that there was a part that missed Jules — even if they couldn't be friends.

I need to know that much.

CHAPTER
27

It was a blistering hot day in early August. Jules and Patsy were running down the street from the Humber Theater at Jane and Bloor, screaming the Beatles' song " A Hard Day's Night" at the top of their lungs. The theater had been packed with kids their age or older, who clapped, jumped up and down, laughed, and screamed throughout *A Hard Day's Night*.

Mrs. Chapman had reluctantly given Jules the money to go. Jules was becoming an expert at getting money out of her – for bus fare, movies, or trips to Cloverdale and the Kingsway. She had a dozen surefire ways to get on Mrs. Chapman's nerves, like turning on the radio in the kitchen full blast when her soaps started. Mrs. Chapman would do anything to get rid of Jules.

Jules was so glad Patsy was back. They played together every day.

"Don't your mom and dad get tired of me being at your place?" Jules asked after playing at Patsy's five days in a row.

"Nah. I don't complain so much about having to look after Marcus."

Jules and Patsy knew the words to every Beatles' song. They listened to Patsy's records and practiced dancing in Patsy's bedroom. Jules hoped they weren't turning into Marilyn and Veronica.

"How great was that movie?" Jules shouted.

"And the music was simply fab! Fab Four fab!"

"But they're funny, too, and . . ." Jules sighed, "perfectly perfect!"

"Paul McCartney is dreamy!"

"You mean John Lennon."

"Paul."

"John."

"Paul."

"John."

They kept shouting out the names of their favorite Beatle back and forth until Patsy grabbed Jules's arm just before the bus stop. "I don't want to get on yet. Let's go down to the park by the Humber."

When they got there, they lay on the grass under a gigantic willow tree.

"It's so fantastic here, almost like a whole other world," said Jules.

"Yes, indeedy," Patsy mumbled with her eyes closed. Suddenly she sat up. "Hey! You've given me a great idea. Let's pretend we don't belong here, or don't know where we are. We go up to people and ask them ridiculous questions."

"I don't know, Patsy. They might get mad."

"Nah. We'll act stupid. C'mon, I'll go first."

They stood up and walked along the path by the river. An old man with his dog came toward them.

"Excuse me," Patsy said. "What planet is this?"

The man looked as if he hadn't heard the question right, and – before he could say anything – Patsy burst out laughing and ran away. Jules stood in front of him for a second more, not knowing what to do, then ran after her.

"Well, you handled that rather well, I must say," Jules said when she caught up to Patsy.

"Must you?"

"I must. Let's see if I can do any better." Jules was never shy when she was playing with Patsy. It was as if she became another person.

They walked along the path again. This time, they came across three teenage girls.

"Here goes," Jules whispered to Patsy. Then, to the girls, she asked, "Excuse me, I know what time it is, but could you tell me what time it isn't?"

The girls looked at each other, puzzled.

When one of them actually looked at her watch, Patsy howled.

"What?" another asked.

"What time isn't it?" Jules repeated.

"Get lost, you little creeps!"

Over the summer, Jules and her father had only one visit. Tracie came, too. It was a beautiful day in August, and they went to High Park. Her dad and Tracie tried not to show it, but Jules could tell they were hungover. All Tracie wanted to do was lie in the shade and sleep it off. Her dad walked with Jules around the park for a while, but she had to play by herself on the kiddie swings for most of the visit.

Early in September, he called to tell her they were going up to Thunder Bay again. "We'll meet up when I get back. But I'll be looking for work, too."

Silence.

"Those dealerships. Too big. Too many bosses."

The usual sinking, sick feeling came over her.

Another job gone.

Another hope gone.

PART THREE

POINT ZERO

CHAPTER
28

*B*eing separate, alienated, doesn't mean falling
off the earth, not being part of it. It's being in
the world — breathing, eating, moving about —
and only that. With no spark, no atom of anything else.
Time is measured by clocks and days. The sun rises and
sets. And people like me are forced to be a part. Forced
to be apart.

Mrs. Chapman took Marilyn and Veronica on a
big shopping spree just before high school started.
The girls said they used their summer wages to pay
for all the clothes, but Jules knew that Veronica was
putting every penny she earned toward buying a car
and Marilyn was saving up to go to Europe with her
class. Mrs. Chapman told Jules that when she started
working, she could buy her own clothes, too.

The only thing Jules wanted was a pair of skates.

Hers were a couple of sizes too small. And when winter set in, she'd be out of luck if she wanted to go to Teresa's or the indoor rink at Montgomery. She asked her new social worker, Suzanne, if she could get a pair.

Eileen had left Children's Aid in June to go back to school. There had been a fill-in, Linda, for a few weeks, but Jules never met her. An invisible social worker would have been better than Suzanne. Eileen kept in touch, even when the news she had for Jules was not what Jules wanted to hear – that her dad didn't always show up for court, that the temporary custody order was being renewed.

Jules could never reach Suzanne by phone at the Children's Aid office. And if Jules left a message, Suzanne never called back right away.

"You're not the only family on my caseload, Jules," Suzanne would say when they finally did connect.

I'd have to be pretty stupid to think that.

Suzanne informed Jules that there was a process to go through if Jules wanted "extras" and that Jules had to be patient. So Jules tried being patient – and ended up with nothing.

The only good thing about September was that Jules would be starting school again, which meant seeing friends every day and being out of the Chapman house.

———

"Here we come! In the whole wide world, you will not find two more fabulous Grade 8-ers!" Patsy shouted as both she and Jules entered the schoolyard on the first day of school.

Katie Adamson was now proudly in Grade 1 at Our Lady of Peace. When Jules bumped into her, she was as bubbly and excited about everything as Jules remembered her to be. She attached herself to Jules like a magnet, acting like a big shot whenever Jules played with her and her friends. Jules still saw Jeff and John around the school, but because of Katie, she didn't go out of her way to avoid them like she used to.

My dad can't get mad at me for it. Mrs. Adamson's kids are innocent bystanders.

Jules often walked home with them, or – if Mr. Adamson was home – she went as far as their street. The Chapmans lived in the opposite direction. Because the kids dawdled a lot on the way, it took hours for Jules to get "home," where she promptly got into trouble.

"Jules Doherty and Marta Kowalsky, to the front!"

Lunch period had ended, and they'd just taken their seats.

"Think you can play tag in the school hallways? Think you can do whatever you want because you're in Grade 8?"

"No, Sister," Jules and Marta replied in unison.

Marta had chased Jules into the school through the side doors, and their squeals of laughter must have annoyed the teachers who were trying to eat their lunch.

Sister Emily, the former principal, would've given them a short lecture and made them stay after class or pick up garbage in the schoolyard. But the new principal, Sister Martha Jane, was something else again. She taught Jules's Grade 8 class, and – in the short time since school started – not one kind word had come out of her mouth.

Sister Martha Jane pulled out the strap from her desk drawer – in slow motion. "Right hand out, Jules." Sister stood as far back from Jules as she could.

Wham! The full weight of Sister's body went into every blow.

Jules wanted to cry out – and would have if she'd hurt herself in the playground.

Then it was Marta's turn.

By the time Sister finished giving them both the strap, Marta looked like she was going to throw up. Tears ran down her cheeks.

"Back to your seats."

Sister swapped the strap for her second-favorite weapon, a yardstick, and started patrolling the aisles, talking about "The Highwayman," a poem they were studying. She liked to tap the yardstick against her palm as she walked, then – pow! – whack it down on a kid's arm or leg when they least expected it.

Jules held herself in. She wasn't going to cry – especially because Sister was looking over at her every now and then, expecting tears to fall. There were some people you didn't show pain to.

If you think your knife-blade eyes can cut into me, you're wrong. You have no idea how tough I am.

Jules got the strap often after that. She'd find out what rules she was supposed to follow and try to obey them – only to find out Sister had made up a new rule and didn't tell anybody about it until someone had broken it. Sister marched down the school hallways like a football player, her hands in fists, ready to whack anybody who got in her way. The white starchy thing under her veil pinched her face, making the fat in her cheeks bulge out. Maybe it made her uncomfortable. Maybe being a nun made her uncomfortable. She was the first nun Jules met who wasn't trying to please God.

"I hate my class. I need to get out of it and go to Miss Davies's Grade 8 class – the one Patsy's in," Jules told Mrs. Chapman one afternoon after school. Asking for something important from Mrs. Chapman was usually a waste of time, but by the beginning of October, Jules felt as if her stomach were being put through a wringer washer when she thought about Sister. She'd already pretended to be sick, though Mrs. Chapman hadn't believed her.

"What a crazy thing to say."

"I'm not going to school then."

"Is that so? Well, Miss High and Mighty, I'm sure you're in that class for a reason. The school decides who goes where, not you or me. So the answer is no. I'm not asking Sister to switch you. Definitely not."

CHAPTER
29

I must . . .
Will my father back to me.
Will him to let me see Mrs. Adamson.
Will Sister to another planet.
Will the Chapmans to the Twilight Zone.
Will myself to grow up so I don't have to be bossed around all the time.

If Sister wasn't strapping, punching, or hitting someone, she was getting at them in other ways. Every time she talked about families, mothers, or fathers, she'd look at Jules, stand near her, or ask her a question.

"Where's your family from, Jules?"

"Canada."

"Of course, but which country before Canada?"

"I don't know."

Laughter.

"Doherty is an Irish name. Did your father's family come from Ireland?"

"I don't know."

"How about your mother?"

"I don't know."

Laughter floated up at Jules, hitting her like Sister's jabs, punches, and slaps.

I need some relief. And if nobody's going to give it to me, I'm going to get it myself.

Jules pretended to go to school one day, but didn't.

She knew how to get to the Kingsway on her own. And by asking bus drivers, she found out how to get as far as Mimico. She got off the bus just past the Queensway, walked up and down Royal York, going in and out of stores, then along some of the side streets. She didn't expect to see her dad or Tracie.

The city felt weird, like a world children weren't supposed to be a part of – a parallel universe carrying on when kids were all at school.

When she got tired, Jules took the bus back to Bloor and walked to the Brentwood Library in the Kingsway, eating her lunch along the way. Only old people and mothers with really young kids were there. Some of the librarians gave her a look that meant she shouldn't be there.

She picked a book – *The Secret Garden* – found a cozy corner near a window, and read in peace.

After a few chapters, she closed the book and

How am I going to get through all the years of being a kid and getting pushed around? How am I going to make it?

By the time Jules got back, Mrs. Chapman was almost frothing at the mouth. "Never in all my years of being a foster parent has this happened to me!"

The school had called, and Mrs. Chapman had been made to look stupid in front of Sister Martha Jane – and Suzanne – for not knowing where Jules had gone.

Hurray!

Mrs. Chapman wanted other people to think she was holy and good. But she was just going through the motions.

Jules stared at the vein in Mrs. Chapman's forehead. It looked like it was going to burst. When Mr. Chapman came home, he joined in the lecturing. Veronica and Marilyn found excuses to be in the kitchen so they could be part of the peanut gallery.

Jules was silent.

"This will never happen again! You're not getting me into trouble with Children's Aid – I can tell you that much!"

"And it's against the law to skip school, in case you didn't know," Mr. Chapman added.

Leave it to grown-ups to make laws to punish the punished.

"I don't know what's the matter with you lately," Mrs. Chapman continued. "You're short-tempered, you fight with the girls, you take off so you don't have to do chores, and you lock yourself in your room. Do you think you can just do what you want – like you're someone special? Sister says you're one of the worst students in the class, that you never do homework . . . never do assignments."

Jules stared at the pattern in Mrs. Chapman's purple and green housedress.

"Listen to me, Jules. Pay attention! You've got high school next year, and if you don't work hard, you'll end up –" She didn't have to finish the sentence.

Jules looked around at their faces.

Go ahead. Keep thinking I'm weak or stupid or a loser. You're wrong. It took guts to do what I did today. And it was worth it. The air felt different, good to breathe, and I was free.

Jules skipped another day of school the following week, then two the week after that. It was hard to stop.

CHAPTER

30

There'd been no visit from her dad in September, though Jules and her dad kept phoning each other.

No visit in October.

He showed up in early November. Sleet stung their faces as Jules clung to him at the Chapmans' front door.

"Hey, hey. What's this?"

She couldn't speak.

"C'mon, Jules, what's wrong?"

Mrs. Chapman's face went red. They were making a scene in front of her neighbors. "People'll start gawking, Jules, and wonder what the drama's all about."

Her dad pretended to laugh, but Jules could tell he didn't think any part of it was funny.

"Where were you, Dad? I couldn't get you on the phone. Don't you want to see me anymore?"

"Come in, Jules, for heaven's sake! The weather's too awful to be standing outside." Mrs. Chapman gave them an angry "you people" kind of look as she practically pulled them through the doorway. "Jules, it's okay. You're going to have a nice visit," she said flatly. "Just go into the living room and be with your father there. It's been a while, I guess." Mrs. Chapman turned to look at Jules's father, then moved quickly away from him. "Well, I'll make some coffee."

Jules's dad walked awkwardly into the living room – Jules was still holding on to him.

"C'mon, Jules. Let go, for Christ's sake!" He smelled of cigarettes and alcohol. His face was pinched with the cold.

They sat in their usual spots on the couch.

"Why didn't you come?"

"I wanted to."

No, you didn't!

"But why not?"

Anger, guilt, sadness moved like shadows across his face.

"I've been in this place almost a year. A year, Dad. It's like prison. I can't take it!" she yelled.

"'Prison'? Bloody hell." He edged farther away from her on the sofa. "You know something? You're getting to be a spoiled little brat. An ungrateful little brat. Look at you! You're warm, clean, got a roof over your head, no worries. I'd give anything to be in your place."

"But —"

"Shut up about it or I'm leaving. You don't understand."

No, I don't.

"Things are tough right now."

When aren't they?

"Where's Tracie?"

"Working."

Mrs. Chapman brought in the coffee.

Jules and her dad sat in silence as Mrs. Chapman set the tray down and left the room. Jules remembered the times they used to drink coffee or tea just to keep warm in their old house.

Beaten down and used up. That's how he looks.

"C'mon, Jules," he said, almost like a kid. "It's such a rotten day out there, let's cheer ourselves up and talk about something else. Before you know it, it'll be Christmas, your favorite time of year. Let's talk about that. What we'll do — you, me, and Tracie? What do you want me to get you for for Christmas?"

It doesn't matter what I want. You never get it.

But Jules decided to try and be in a better mood to please him. "A Beatles record."

"The Beatles? Those hairy creeps?" he said, laughing.

"Dad?"

"Hmm?"

"Christmas'll be wonderful together."

CHAPTER

31

"Jules Doherty – one."

Jules couldn't help but smile as Sister Martha Jane looked at her with disgust. She walked up to the front of the class and collected her box of doughnuts.

Every year, the kids at school had to sell chocolates, raffle tickets, or something else to raise money for supplies or equipment nobody ever saw once the money came in. Doughnuts were the moneymaker that year. Every kid had to go door to door in their neighborhood, signing people up for as many boxes as they could.

Sister finished reading out the names of students and their doughnut counts. She wanted her class to sell the most and kept saying they had to set a good example for the rest of the school.

Hah! I couldn't care less. The only thing I want to do is eat as many of those doughnuts as I can before giving the box to Mrs. Chapman.

Mrs. Chapman had sprung for only a dozen – and complained about having to do that much.

They were dismissed early to trudge through the streets with their deliveries. Jules first walked to the Grade 1 classroom, at the far end of the school, because she'd promised to help Katie.

Katie's class was empty, so Jules went outside to look for her. Kids were streaming out of school, heading off in all directions, but a small crowd was standing in a circle just beyond the back exit doors, almost out of sight. When Jules got close enough, she could see that Katie was in the middle, looking frightened. The bully from her old class, Jerry Chambers, was standing over Katie and passing around an open box of doughnuts. Another box lay on the ground.

Jules pushed herself through the circle, snatched the box from Jerry, and handed it to Katie.

"Give it back, foster girl."

Laughter.

"Make me."

Jules rarely got into fights. When Jerry or another bully picked on her, especially when they teased her about being in foster care, she'd turn herself off and try to feel nothing.

Maybe they think I'm a coward.

Jerry was the kind of bully who acted like a goody-two-shoes in front of teachers and played mean tricks on kids behind their backs.

Katie bent down awkwardly to pick up the box on the ground. Jerry made a move to kick it away. Jules jabbed him in the ribs as hard as she could. He lost his balance and fell to the ground.

More laughter.

Jerry got back on his feet and came at Jules. She quickly dropped her schoolbag and box of doughnuts to the pavement. With both arms out, Jules rushed toward him and pushed him hard, knocking him down again.

He looked up at her as if he'd never seen her before. Getting up slowly, he turned to face the school. "I hear Crazy Jane. We'd better split."

Sister Martha Jane's name was enough to send everybody running.

"What am I gonna do?" Katie wailed. A large tear rolled down her cheek.

Jules picked up her own box of doughnuts. "Take mine, Katie. Your other box is okay." She opened it to show her. "See? The cardboard's crunched up a bit, but the doughnuts are fine."

"But you'll be in trouble."

"Nah. My doughnuts were just for me."

"All of 'em?"

"Yeah," Jules lied.

"I'll pay you back."

"No, Katie. Forget it."

Jeff and John came out of the school then, deep in conversation, and joined Jules and Katie. They were weighed down with their own boxes and schoolbags.

"A mean, rotten, lousy big kid grabbed a box of my doughnuts," Katie said excitedly. "And Jules beat him up!"

"It didn't happen quite like that. C'mon, you guys. If Sister does come out, *we'll* be the ones in trouble."

"Jules, Jules," Katie shrieked as she spotted her in the school lineup the next morning. "A letter from Mom."

"A what?"

Katie pushed an envelope at Jules just as the bell rang. "See you at recess!"

Jules stuffed the envelope in her schoolbag. She didn't dare open it in class − Sister might take it. Jules waited until lunchtime.

"Thank you so much for what you did, Jules. Katie looked up to you before. You're her hero now. Mine, too. Sophie Adamson."

Scotch-taped to the note was money for a dozen doughnuts.

Jules went to bed that night, her heart aglow.

CHAPTER
3 2

December 9. Wednesday.

"Remember, Jules," said Mrs. Chapman, "Suzanne's coming after school. Make sure you're here by four o'clock."

Argh.

Jules dragged herself home. Her report card had been a disaster. She was in for it now.

It would've been easier to face the sermon if Eileen was giving it. Jules didn't like Suzanne. She was short, with a square body, square head, square face, and sour expression. She talked down to Jules — or around her to Mrs. Chapman. She always acted as if whatever Sister Martha Jane or Mrs. Chapman said mattered most. So Jules didn't say anything to Suzanne if she could help it. Suzanne wasn't on her side.

"Hi, Jules," Mrs. Chapman called out cheerfully when Jules came into the house.

Suzanne must be here.

She put her things away and went to the kitchen.

"How are you, Jules?"

I know you don't care, Suzanne.

"Okay."

"How's school?"

Sister beat up a bunch of us today. My hands and arms are still sore, stinging. In a real rage, she was.

"Okay."

"Jules, are you hungry? Do you want a snack?" Mrs. Chapman asked in her fake voice.

"No."

"How about you, Suzanne? Would you like some coffee? And cookies, maybe?"

Suzanne smiled. "Yes, that'll be nice."

Jules could tell she liked being waited on and made to feel important. Mrs. Chapman was good at that.

Suzanne asked a few more idiotic questions about how Jules was doing. Jules sat and stared at her or mumbled non-answers. She was getting to be an expert at answering questions without actually saying anything. It didn't take long before Suzanne was good and frustrated.

When Mrs. Chapman served the coffee, Suzanne took some time to add cream and sugar, comment on the cookies, and make small talk about Christmas. Then she sighed, took a few sips, put her mug down, helped herself to a cookie, looked in her briefcase, brought out a file of papers, and started reading them.

"I've got something to tell you, Jules. Your father, your dad . . . um, there was a court date in early November."

Stupid court.

"He didn't show up. Even before that, we tried to contact him. You had a scheduled visit . . . um . . ." Suzanne kept looking through her papers. "Your visits are for once a week. . . ."

No, Dad. No.

Suzanne shifted papers in her file, reading parts of them to herself, putting others aside. She didn't look at Jules once.

"Did he say anything about going somewhere, getting a new place, when you had your last visit?"

Dad. Oh, Dad.

"When was the last time — oh, here it is. You saw him in November, just over a month ago." Suzanne chewed on her cookie as she spoke, slowly raising her sour eyes to Jules. "And over the summer, just one visit."

Help me.

"We haven't been able to reach him for some time, Jules. We don't know where he is." Suzanne put the papers down. She spoke slowly and deliberately as she delivered the smack-down punch. "I've been to Tracie's. She's gone, too, I'm afraid. Left her rooming house. No one's sure when. They didn't give notice. We've gone to your dad's last place of work, asked everybody who knew them, but . . . it seems as if he's left the city."

A tear escaped.

"Did your father say anything about moving? Do you have any idea where they might have gone?"

Going, going, gone.

"I know it's hard, but we have to talk about this. You know your dad best."

No, I don't. Yes, I do.

Suzanne was trying to put the right amount of concern into her face and voice, but Jules could tell that a part of her − deep down − liked being "the god" in people's lives.

Jules stood up quickly and knocked over Suzanne's mug. Coffee spilled on all the papers. She ran out of the room, up the stairs, and threw herself on the bed.

Suzanne came up after her. "Please, Jules. I don't want to upset you, but I have to tell you what's going on. You're not a child; you'll be thirteen soon. . . ."

Dad. Oh, Dad.

"Jules, we'll do everything we can to find him."

"Get out!" Jules screamed.

"Jules, ple −"

"Get out! Get out!"

Suzanne wouldn't leave. She was trying to come up with social-worker words to calm Jules down.

Jules got up from the bed, pushed Suzanne into the hallway, and slammed the door shut. "Leave me alone. Everybody, just leave me alone!"

Jules could hear Mrs. Chapman charge up the stairs, spouting words of comfort that had never come out of her mealy mouth before. "Oh, you poor thing. Jules, honey —"

"Go away!" Sobs choked Jules, making it harder to scream. "Get out. Get out of my life. All of you!"

She got Maggie out of her hiding spot and curled up on the bed, listening to her own cries as if she were not in her own body. Through the torment, she heard the voices of the two women in the hallway. Eventually they went downstairs.

I hate you. All of you. Hate!

Jules cried and screamed until her voice was ragged and her lungs hurt. Pain shot through her stomach and chest, and a voice in her head cut into every thought.

He's gone. He's gone. He's gone. What am I going to do? Oh, help me. Somebody, help me! He doesn't want me. I was right all along. Right, right, right. He doesn't want this piece of garbage that's Jules.

Exhausted and shivering, she pulled Maggie closer — tight, tight — under the blankets. No one tried to come into her room or talk to her. She fell asleep and didn't wake up until morning.

Jules felt numb. She had nothing left inside.

She got out of bed and knelt by the window, looking out at the street.

Over the past year, she'd learned that she could keep going like other people as long as she believed it was possible for her and her dad to be together. There wasn't any point now.

She'd understood all along – what it meant when he'd make excuses for not visiting, when his visits happened just every two weeks, once a month, then not at all.

There's no one for me. I might as well disappear.

CHAPTER
3 3

Mrs. Chapman knocked on the door around eight o'clock. When Jules didn't answer, she opened it, staring into the room. Jules didn't turn around.

Don't waste your time. I'm not really here.

"I'm not going to school."

"But —"

"Go away."

"Aren't you coming down for breakfast?"

"No."

"Look. I know you're upset, hon. It's really tough, but . . ."

But nothing. You don't know how it feels and you never will.

"Why don't you come down? I'll make something good."

I'm not going to speak. Silence is one of the few weapons I have.

Sometime later, Jules got dressed, grabbed her schoolbag, snuck downstairs and out the back door.

Let them worry – if they worry at all. The only reason the Chapmans are concerned is because they've got to answer to Children's Aid.

Jules got on the bus and found her way to Mimico. She walked up and down the snowy streets all day long. When it started to get dark, she took the bus to the library and pretended to read until closing time.

I can't go back to the Chapmans. I won't.

Churches are open all night. They're sanctuaries and can't kick people out.

Our Lady of Sorrows was nearby, but she'd get there too early.

If I walk all the way to Our Lady of Peace church, it'll be late when I get there. Nobody will be around.

Walking alone in the dark didn't frighten her.

When she got to the church, she entered through the side door, walked down the narrow right aisle to a middle pew, and sat down. After her eyes adjusted to the darkness, she stared at the altar for minutes, an hour, two hours.

And when she could no longer sit up, she emptied out her schoolbag and used it as a pillow so she could lay her body out. Yellow stars, set against a blue plaster sky, dotted the church ceiling – high, high up.

I'm tired. So tired.

———

"And what do you think you're doing?"

Jules was startled by the voice and nearly fell to the floor.

Where am I?

Light streamed through stained glass windows.

Morning.

It was busybody Bendinelli, the elderly woman who lived next door to Patsy and came to pray at church every day. "Did you hear what I said?"

Think fast.

"Uh . . . I just came in here before school. Must've dozed off."

"Then why aren't you wearing your uniform?"

"It got ripped . . . I have to wear my regular clothes."

Mrs. Bendinelli didn't buy it. "You stay right where you are, young lady. Father Matthews is going to hear about this."

"No, don't. Please."

Jules frantically pushed her things into her bag and ran out of the church.

CHAPTER
3 4

"Get in here. Sit down in that damn chair, and if you so much as move a muscle, I'll call the police on you myself," Mrs. Chapman yelled. "They were in this very kitchen! Did you know that? The police cruiser was parked on the street for all the neighbors to see! What nerve. What colossal, stinking nerve. You're going to pay for what you've done. There are consequences. Sit down in that chair, I said!" Mrs. Chapman pushed Jules down into a kitchen chair and reached for the phone. "Let's see what Suzanne has to say!"

"I haven't eaten . . . can I –"

"You cannot. Be still and keep your mouth shut." Mrs. Chapman looked as if she was prepared to sit on top of Jules if necessary.

Suzanne arrived at nine o'clock.

"Just get her things and take her away," Mrs. Chapman said as soon as Suzanne stepped inside the kitchen.

"Eleanor, I know you're upset."

"Do you now?"

"Jules, why don't you go upstairs? I'll come up in a minute," Suzanne said.

"You will do no such thing. The only place she's going is out that door."

"But it's Christmastime, Eleanor. You know how hard it is to place –"

"I don't care. Why should I, after the past twenty-four hours?"

"I know. It's been –"

"Terrible? Awful? No. Hell is what it is – having a twelve-year-old child who's capable of doing something like this. The police were here. In! My! House!"

"It was such a shock, finding out about her father."

"Give me a break. That bum? Like she didn't know what was going on with him. You can't call *him* a father. Boozing all the time. Never working. Never visiting."

"Please. Let's not talk –"

"About Jules and Joe Doherty? What they are? He's a drunk, and she's going to be a juvenile delinquent. She's always in a silent rage, snapping at everybody. Skips school, as you know very well, and is going to fail this year. Barricades herself in that room, which is a mess. Won't help around the house, do chores. How many times have I told you all this, Suzanne? The sooner she's out of here, the better. There's no family life for us with her around!"

"Eleanor! Jules, why don't you —"

"She's not moving! She goes into the girls' room all the time. Who knows what's missing? And I worry she'll take her anger out on them. I never told Eileen this, but she tore up one of the dresses they gave her and stuffed the pieces in the garbage. Thought I didn't notice, Jules? I mean, really! And what is she capable of if she can stay out all night?"

Mrs. Chapman threw her arms into the air. She was wild, frantic.

"I'm not going to be responsible. Looking after babies was tough, but that was nothing compared to this. And the girls. My precious girls. They wanted her out even before this happened. No. She's got to go."

"Eleanor, she can't hear . . . she shouldn't —"

Jules stood up. Despite the harshness of Mrs. Chapman's words, it was strangely satisfying to see Mrs. Chapman act like her real self to an outsider.

"She's a liar," Jules said scornfully. "A phony, a money-grubbing witch —"

"Jules! Stop!" Suzanne commanded.

"See?" Mrs. Chapman yelled. "That's just what you can expect from a worthless piece of trash."

"Stop! It's time to calm down, Eleanor. Jules, let's go upstairs."

Suzanne grabbed Jules's arm and led her out of the kitchen.

"Yes. Better get me out of here," Jules said, looking back contemptuously at Mrs. Chapman. "Or I'll show you just how rotten I really am!"

CHAPTER
35

December 11. One year gone by.

A million years gone by.

The emergency home was off Dundas Street, near the Cloverdale Mall. It was as noisy and chaotic as Mrs. Currie's home. Two other foster kids were staying there.

Suzanne told Jules she was going to have to tell potential foster parents about her behavior and the bad relationship she'd had with the Chapmans. She warned Jules that if she didn't smarten up, it'd be hard to place her. She went on and on, trying to make Jules feel guilty.

There's only one thing I care about.

"How'll my dad find me?"

"Jules, I thought you were smarter than that. All he has to do is contact Children's Aid."

"But what if he doesn't? What if he phones or

goes to the Chapmans' and I'm not there?"

"They'll let him know what's happened."

I bet they will.

The only good thing to come out of the last few days was that Jules didn't have to put up with Sister Martha Jane. The Christmas holidays were starting soon, and she might have to transfer to a new school after Children's Aid found her another foster home.

December 12. Saturday.

It was just getting light out. Jules put on lots of clothes, went downstairs before anyone was up, quietly found her coat and boots, and left the house.

I'm getting good at this.

*It's better to be outside. My sadness can spread out —
into the open air.*

It was too bright. Everything seemed too alive. Even though it was early, people were out walking or rushing around in their cars as if they belonged somewhere.

She walked over to Bloor, caught a bus, and got off at the library, where she spent the next few hours reading and dozing.

About one-thirty, she got to the Six Points Plaza. Christmas lights and decorations brightened the storefronts. Once again, a small Christmas tree forest had sprung up in the parking lot.

How familiar everything looks. But how different. It's still me, Jules, staring out at the world, but I've changed. Everything's changed.

She began pacing up and down in front of Zellers. She didn't want to stay there, didn't want to leave.

Why can't I just disappear, dissolve, like a mirage?

Jules put her face to the glass and held a hand to either side to hold back the glare of the sun.

"Hi, Jules." Mrs. Adamson's voice.

How did she see me?

"Hi," Jules mumbled, turning back to face the glass.

"How've you been?"

Jules turned to face Mrs. Adamson, but couldn't bring herself to look up. "Uh, okay. I guess."

The truth of a lie.

"You don't . . . you look awfully thin."

Stop! Please!

"How's your dad?"

Tears started to form, but Jules smothered them. "Um . . . he's . . ."

Panic. What can I say? Stupid, stupid father.

"I don't know." Jules almost spit the words out. "He took off again." She looked up into Mrs. Adamson's face and saw what she'd wanted to see: Mrs. Adamson missed her.

Time to go, time to go.

"Oh, Jules." Mrs. Adamson tried to touch her arm.

Jules pushed her away, almost knocking her over. But Mrs. Adamson just stood there, looking as if Jules had been the one to get hurt.

"Don't blame yourself."

You don't know anything about it!

But as she looked at Mrs. Adamson, Jules knew – had always known – that Mrs. Adamson understood somehow.

She had to get out of there – and ran.

Back to nothing. Over to nothing. Around to nothing.

When Jules returned to the emergency home, she went up to the room assigned to her, pulled out Maggie from her suitcase, and rocked back and forth on the bed.

My dad is never coming back to me.

He's gone. And even though I'm a foster kid, somehow – because I can eat and sleep and go to school and live in a warm house with people who don't drink or fight like we do, who work or go to school like people are supposed to – he's convinced himself that that's enough for me, that it's better than the life I had with him.

Maybe it's because he never had enough of those things himself. And other needs don't count. Especially if you're poor. Especially if you're an alcoholic.

An alcoholic.

Jules had never been able to admit that to herself before. But she'd always known.

Because he's an alcoholic, all his money and time and all of himself go into that. There's no room for anything else. Anyone else. Loving him doesn't seem to matter.

If I hurt myself, jump off a bridge, stand in front of a truck, or swallow some garbage, I'd fall off the face of the earth. No one cares enough to notice me doing it. Forget about why. And, in the end, there isn't anyone who cares enough to be sad once I'm gone.

Her thoughts went round and round in a dark hard groove. Eventually, she'd get stuck in it and never get out.

No.

On Monday, Jules went back to the Six Points Plaza, walked into Zellers, and headed to the toy department. She made room for herself at the book display and started to read.

It wasn't long before Mrs. Adamson came over to speak to her and back into her life.

CHAPTER
36

The name Sophie means "wisdom." Jules looked it up.

Wisdom came into her life in the form of a woman with X-ray vision, a superhero, with superpowers nobody ever talked about.

Jules spent Christmas with the Adamsons. Soon she began visiting regularly, staying overnight and even for entire weekends. Being in their home was awkward and strange at first. But being with the Adamsons wasn't like staying at the Chapmans'. The minute she walked through their door, Jules knew that.

One night in the middle of January, Sophie — she'd told Jules to call her and Frank by their first names — asked Jules to come over for dinner. When she arrived, Sophie told her that Katie, Jeff, and John were at their grandma's.

What's wrong? What have I done?

Jules could barely eat during dinner.

"I guess you're wondering what's up?" Frank said when they were on dessert.

Jules was too nervous to answer him.

"We've talked about it with the kids, and . . . we'd love it if . . . we know it's not an easy decision. . . ." Sophie stammered.

"Sophie," Frank said softly. "Shall I?"

Sophie shook her head with a dermined "no."

"I don't know what foster care's like, Jules," Sophie said. "But I lost my mom when I was seven. Never had a father to speak of. I was put in a home in England, where I was born, then shipped off to Canada when I was eight. I was adopted and sent to a farm. I know what it's like . . ." Sophie looked as if she was struggling not to cry ". . . when parents are gone, to be sent away when you're just a child. But most of all, I know what it's like to feel as if nobody wants you." She stopped.

Jules was shaken by the look on Sophie's face.

"That's why, Jules," Frank said, "we wanted to ask you – to make sure it's what you want – if Sophie and I could become your foster parents?"

There it is. There it is.

"It'll take time to process the paperwork. But the most important thing is, we need to know you *want* to be here, with us," Frank said.

Sophie was smiling now. "If the kids had their way, you'd be here tomorrow."

"I can't think of any other twelve-year-old girl in the whole of Toronto we'd rather have as part of our family." Those last words came so easily to Frank.

"Will you think about it?" Sophie asked.

Jules was secretly glad the Adamsons wanted her to take her time making a decision. The life she'd imagined for herself with her father was over, smashed into a million pieces, but she wanted Suzanne to keep looking for him. She needed to find him, to know why he didn't want her.

There was another reason, though, and it was connected to the first.

Maybe the Adamsons will get rid of me, too. People don't ignore a child completely or throw them away if that child is really good or worth anything.

Jules never said those exact words to Sophie, but in one way or another, Jules tried to make her understand that there had to be something wrong with her.

Jules's true self had been disappearing, bleeding out of her for so long that she didn't know who she was anymore.

"I wish there was a mirror," Sophie said one day, "like the one in *Snow White*. And you could ask it, 'Mirror, mirror, on the wall, who's the fairest of them all?' And it would tell you who was fair all right — but on the inside. And I'd hold that mirror up to you, and there it would be, the radiant soul of Jules Doherty. For you to see with your own eyes."

And then they both laughed. Jules thought maybe Sophie said it as a joke, but Sophie said things like that to her own kids all the time.

Jules never forgot.

CHAPTER

37

The Adamson house wasn't far from where Jules and her dad used to live. Sometimes she'd go and look at the back of her old place, from the park. Another family lived there now.

She thought about how she'd always been cold and hungry when she and her dad lived there. Over the years, most places they'd lived in had been cold and ugly.

Jules knew that being poor made life cold and ugly. It made people that way, too – but not always. The Adamsons were poor and their house might look ugly to some, but nothing else about them was like that. Nothing.

When she was with them, Jules felt happy. Over time, she could say that to herself without feeling like she was betraying her father.

A permanent bed was set up for her in Katie's room, when she moved in at Easter. She never understood why Katie had become attached to her so quickly, following her around everywhere. And why Katie, a child herself, was always worried about Jules.

Jules played with Katie and the twins to her heart's content. As Gypsies, knights, kings and queens, secret agents, superheroes, army generals, spies, villains, magicians, wizards and sorcerers, explorers, dragon slayers, and astronauts, they went on wild adventures in the park nearby or around the house on rainy days – "forever-together," as Katie said. They treated Jules as the oldest, the one to look up to.

Unbelievable.

And, even then, Jules couldn't prevent some of the feelings that rose up.

It hurts to see how easy they breathe, in and out, without jagged thoughts. I'll never be like them. There are cuts and holes in me.

The hard part was expressing some of her thoughts and feelings to Sophie and Frank. It was difficult to unravel them.

Talking about my old life – about having to leave my dad, my home, what I went through at the Chapmans' – is all stuck in hurt. But keeping it inside will never do me any good. Holding on to the bad is like holding on to an infection. It ends up hurting more.

Talking about her father was the hardest thing of all.

Sophie and Frank might think what everybody else does – that he's scum. Alcoholic scum. I hate the word "alcoholic." Hate all that it is. Hate my father. Love him.

CHAPTER
38

Suzanne is there, in the kitchen.
Sophie and Frank are, too.
Why are they all here — on a school day?
But high school's great. I'm doing okay.
Those are the thoughts I had. Nothing more.
I should have known. Should have felt a difference inside, in the air I breathe. But I didn't. I didn't.
Suzanne stood up right away. "Tracie called us from Vancouver, Jules. I'm so sorry, but your father . . ."
Even then I didn't feel it, didn't believe it. It wasn't possible even to say the word. My father couldn't be dead.
Tracie told Suzanne they'd gone to Vancouver so that Jules's dad could find what was left of his family.
Family.
The next few months went out of memory. If Sophie hadn't held Jules to the ground, grief would have spun her off the earth.

There was no reason, after that, not to love her. Not to love them all.

"Jewels, jewels, jewels, jewels," Katie chants as she climbs up and down, over and around me just before we go to bed. She always spells my name that way, even though I tell her it isn't right.

She falls asleep with as many of her dolls as she can fit onto her pillow, one human head among the strange and fantastical ones. It makes me smile just to watch her.

I keep my own doll safe. I'll care for Maggie always and — one day — give her to my own child. I'll tell her what she means to me and why I love her so.

As I lie here in our room, waiting for sleep, I can almost feel my body grow, cell by cell, stretching into the night air. There's room for me to do that here, enough love to let me come back to the person I was, to fill out into the person I want to be.

I told Sophie about my nightmare.

When there's no light in our lives, Sophie said, we hunger for it — any living thing is the same. It's what we need, like air to breathe, water to drink.

I am like any living thing.

I am not a shadow being.

I am not a shadow girl.